Snorkel McCorkle
and the
Lost Flipper

A Musical Book

written by
Linda R. Thornburg

based on characters by
Katherine Archer

music and lyrics by
Katherine Archer

A
Snorkel
McCorkle
Book

A Snorkel McCorkle Book

First Edition, Book with Music, May 2020

Published as an e-book

Published by Belles Lettres, Inc.

First Print Edition, Book with Music, September 2021

Published by Belles Lettres, Inc.

Snorkel McCorkle and the Lost Flipper

Copyright © Linda Rose Thornburg and

Catherine Ann Curtis (aka Katherine Archer), 2021

All rights reserved

Paperback Edition, A Musical Book, September 2021, Belles Lettres, Inc.

Based on *Snorkel McCorkle,* Screenplay

with music, lyrics and text

Copyright © Linda Rose Thornburg and

Catherine Ann Curtis (aka Katherine Archer), 2018

Snorkel McCorkle Song Collection, Volume 1

Copyright © Catherine Ann Curtis, 2015

Snorkel McCorkle Song Collection, Volume 2

Copyright © Catherine Ann Curtis

and Linda Rose Thornburg, 2018

All rights reserved

ISBN: 978-0-578-71791-3

LINKS TO MUSIC

This book was originally published as an iBook with music.
We had many requests from friends to publish
Snorkel McCorkle and the Lost Flipper
as a print book.
Adding the music stumped us until we discovered
that QR Code technology could help.
You can stream the music live
while you read the lyrics in the book.
Whenever you see this QR Code,
scan it and play the song listed in the text.

*Snorkel McCorkle Song Page
entire Album*

There are also QR codes for links to web page references.

While we think the iBook is the best format,
we hope you will enjoy this printed version as well!
If you do not have a QR code reader,
the music can be accessed through the hyperlink:
https://www.reverbnation.com/SnorkelMccorkle

Dedicated to

Mary Elizabeth McCorkle Kirk

Amy McCorkle Kirk

and

Betty Rose Thornburg

Acknowledgments

We gratefully acknowledge all of the talented people who helped bring Snorkel McCorkle to life. They include Michelle Lodge, whose vibrant illustrations of our heroine and her friends leap from the page, and Duffy Bishop and Chris Carlson, whose unique voices and musical styles round out the characters of Matilda and Figaro. Thanks, Chris, for time in your studio, as well. Thanks to Fox Hillyer for the saxophone riffs and musical farts!

Thanks to Janet Mullaney, for her editing expertise and infinite support, and to Tom Thornburg, for his eye for detail. Thanks to Mabel Maney for her encouragement. Thanks to Rob Heath and Sapna Batish for their scientific knowledge and for reading drafts. Thanks to Toni and Denny Hawthorn for taking such good care of Kat and Cappie. Thanks to Charon Luebbers, Gloria Danvers, Catherine Heymsfeld, Sally Procaccini, Robert Curtis, Dean Scott Waters and Zen Green for unstinting support. Thanks to Kenny Holliday and Kris Lee-Scott for technical notes. Thanks to Gwen Taylor, Julie Novak, MaryJo Martin, Tracy Colson and Zelda for inspiration. Thanks to Roman and Lara for reading the first chapters and encouraging us to continue.

A special thank you goes to all of the people working tirelessly to save this beautiful blue-green sphere we call home. You inspire us daily. We hope our Snorkel will educate and inspire a new generation of eco-warriors.

TABLE of CONTENTS

Chapter 1:
Snorkel McCorkle

Flaaaap. Slaaaap. Flaaaap. Slaaaap. Snorkel's mismatched flippers—one blue, one yellow—slapped rhythmically against the tiles as she made her way through the grocery aisle with her dad. Through the oval filter of her pink diving mask she looked at cereal boxes, stacks of produce, and the dairy case. The sound of her breathing through the snorkel filled her head so she couldn't hear the whispered disdain of the women she was passing.

"Poor child," said the first woman.

"Poor father," snorted the second.

"He just can't handle that child. Look at her hair!"

"Someone should call children's services," retorted the first.

Snorkel's dad, a ginger-haired man in his late 30s, was still in green scrubs from his shift in the ER. Dr. Sean McCorkle held Snorkel's small cocoa brown hand tightly in his large white one and his head high as they passed the snickering women. As if a child wearing a diving mask, snorkel and mis-matched fins through the supermarket were the most normal occurrence in the world. Snorkel McCorkel was ten years old and underwater, but her dad knew she would surface when she was ready.

~~~

The pink snorkel appeared first, then the red corkscrew curls spiraling in all directions from the diving mask perched on top of her head. Snorkel peered around her bedroom door into the upstairs hallway. Her dad was still asleep and she wanted to keep it that way. She slipped out the door and crept down the steps holding her flippers, so she wouldn't make any flapping sounds on the stairs. At the bottom she put them on and adjusted her mask. Grabbing her plastic water bottle and an apple from the fridge she headed out the back door, careful not to let it slam. She had a lot to do this morning.

~~~

A fish startled and darted away when Snorkel's mask and face plunged into the canal. "Oh, sorry," she bubbled. "I didn't mean to frighten you." The fish turned and looked back at her. A school of small fish passed just in front of her mask.

"Hello" rose with the bubbles from her lips. The fish seemed to bubble back. Snorkel was certain they were saying, "Good Morning." She pulled her head from the water and lay back on the wooden boat dock behind her house. She gazed up at the sky. It was going to be a beautiful day. Two pelicans skimmed by. An anhinga squawked overhead and landed on the upright post of the neighbor's dock. Snorkel squawked back. The anhinga squawked again. Then Snorkel. Then the anhinga replied. Snorkel smiled at their exchange. She loved all the creatures of the sea and sky, and they loved her.

Sometimes Snorkel felt like her life was a movie. She was in her life and watching the movie of it at the same time. It was like she was both the camera and the heroine. She couldn't explain it really. Sometimes she could even hear her own theme song playing.

Snorkel McCorkle
Sung by
Katherine Archer

(Scan to start music.)

She's got her mask.
Got her fins.
Got her snorkel, too.
  She just can't wait
for the day to begin.
Got a lot of things to
do.

She loves the water.
She loves the sky.
All the swimmin' finned creatures
And the ones who fly.
Earth's itty bity critters and the big
    ones too!
Gonna help 'em all. Got a lot to do.

Snorkel McCorkle
Never stops movin'
Always on the go.
Snorkel McCorkle
Ready for adventure
Lookin' high and low.
Snorkel McCorkle
The planet's favorite friend.

She's a bit of a diva
A bit of a geek
She swears the animals can speak.
So charismatic,
But her hair's a mess.

Got tangled up in her mask,
I guess.
Snorkel McCorkle
Never stops movin'
Always on the go
Snorkel McCorkle
Ready for adventure
Lookin' high and low.
Snorkel McCorkle.
The planet's favorite...
Friends like her forever true
Will see you through.
Friends like her
Will always be around
She'll never let you down.

So grab your snorkel,
Put on your fins.
Get ready for a beautiful
day to begin.

Snorkel McCorkle
Never stops movin'
Always on the go.
Snorkel McCorkle
Ready for adventure
Lookin' high and low.
Snorkel McCorkle
The planet's favorite friend.
She's our favorite friend.

11

Snorkel kept her kayak at the side of the house under the purple bougainvillea. She had seen a possum hiding there last weekend. It was waiting to get some of the cat's kibbles, but the possum wasn't there today. Carefully Snorkel pulled the kayak from under the bush and dragged it across the grass to the dock. She put on her life vest, put the kayak in the water, and climbed in. The canal behind her house connected to the Tolomato River. As part of the Intracoastal Waterway, the Tolomato flowed into the Matanzas River. At the St. Augustine Inlet, it flowed into the great Atlantic Ocean. It was a perfect day for an adventure on the river.

As Snorkel paddled the kayak through the canal, she took in everything. The last part of the canal snaked through a salt marsh to the river. The tides had been high and the ibises were still nesting. High tides meant plenty of fish and blue crabs for them to feed their chicks, but the eggs would wash away if the tides were too high. Snorkel made a video of a ground nest close to the canal where three brown chicks with their striped bills were chirping for a handout. She had been recording this nest since the ibis had built it, first with its eggs and now with chicks. Snorkel loved this stretch of the marsh. Wherever the ibis stirred up the muddy bottom with their long curled bills, egrets and roseate spoonbills soon followed.

She paddled south onto the Tolomato River. Just then from behind the Bucys' pier charged Brad Bucy on his jet ski. He sped past her creating as big a wake as he could. Then he hung a U-ie and headed back. Just behind him came Brian, Brad's younger brother, on his own jet ski, headed for the opposite side of Snorkel's kayak. The boys were so close in age and looks that people often mistook them for twins. Brad was in Snorkel's class at school. He bullied everyone. Brian was a bully in training. The Bucy brothers circled around Snorkel churning up the water until her kayak overturned, dumping her in the drink. Luckily she was wearing her life vest, fins and mask.

She popped out of the water and swam to the kayak "Can't you read! It's a no wake zone!" she sputtered. Indeed, the sign was posted along the water's edge, just across from the Bucy's pier.

~~~

A scraping noise came from the dumpster in the alley behind the marina. Suddenly, a broken fishing pole flew out of the dumpster, followed by two dented aluminum tent poles, a ball of twine, four plastic milk jugs, and some torn sailcloth. Like a periscope, the pink snorkel emerged from inside the dumpster followed by two hands and a blue flipper, then the yellow flipper. Snorkel climbed over the lip of the dumpster onto a stack of crates and jumped onto the ground.

She gathered her treasures, adjusted her mask and took off up the alley.

In the canal behind Snorkel's house, a large white pelican with a mangled foot dove for a fish, causing a huge splash. The ripples lapped against the wooden dock and outboard motor- boat tied there, but Snorkel didn't notice. She was too busy fashioning the treasure she had gathered from the dumpster into an outrigger for her kayak.

Snorkel was wrapping duct tape around the handles of the milk jugs to secure them to one of the tent poles. Having torn too long a piece of tape to wind, she tangled it in her hair. She managed to tear it from the milk jug, only to have it fly up towards her head and snag another curl. As she freed the first curl, the tape wound round yet another, until it was hopelessly matted in a nest of curls. Snorkel sighed and went back to her task. She would deal with that later.

Satisfied with her creation, Snorkel attached the finished outrigger to the side of her kayak with Velcro. It was a masterpiece. One tent pole was attached to the kayak, and the flexible fishing rod pieces were secured to each end. They were connected over the water to the second tent pole which held the four-gallon milk jugs as buoys.

~~~

Snorkel's dad was cooking dinner when Snorkel entered the kitchen.

"Hey, Dad. What's for dinner?"

"Chicken strips, applesauce and green salad," he replied as he turned to look at her.

"Snorkel! What's that mess in your hair?"

"Just some duct tape. I was…"

"I don't even need to know. Come here and let me try to get that out without having to shave you bald!" Snorkel hopped onto a stool at the end of the counter.

"Ow! Ouch! Ow!" she cried, even though her dad was trying ever so gently to undo the tangle.

"It's all wound up in your mask and snorkel, too. You're gonna have to take them off."

14

"Oh no, Dad. I can't. You know I can't." Snorkel started to panic. Her dad put his arms around her.

"It's okay, Snork. You can put them right back on. I promise." Snorkel reluctantly let him pull the duct tape from the snorkel and mask and then take them off, so he could get to the rest of the tape tangled in her hair. Snorkel clutched them to her chest like the life savers they were.

Snorkel's dad was as inept with the tape stuck in Snorkel's hair as she had been. Every time he freed a small piece of hair another seemed to take its place.

Finally he took a pair of scissors from the drawer. "I'm so sorry, Snorkel. But there doesn't seem to be any other way," he said, snipping both the tape and the curl wound in it from Snorkel's head. "I wish I had paid more attention to what your mom did with your hair," he sighed. "She was the only one who knew what to do with it."

"That's okay Dad," said Snorkel, looking at the tape and curl. "I have so much hair, no one will notice that this piece is missing. Especially with my mask and snorkel on." She slipped them back onto her head and sighed.

Her dad kissed the top of her head and murmured, "My dear Snork. You are so very brave."

Snorkel had put her mask and snorkel on three months ago and had not taken them off since.

Chapter 2:
Tragedy off the Florida Keys

THREE MONTHS EARLIER:

Kelsey McCorkel, Snorkel's mom, a lean 35-year-old of African descent, climbed up the ladder on the side of the marine research boat. She and a crew of three other marine biologists were doing routine water sampling off the Florida Keys. She handed the samples she had just taken to Carlos Rodriguez, a member of the science team, and pushed up her mask. "Carlos, how come you brought me up so soon? I wasn't quite finished."

The crew's Captain, Heather Makepeace, nodded toward the storm clouds approaching from the Gulf, which covered most of the western sky. The sea was getting rougher. "Came outa nowhere," said the Captain. "It's going to be a bad one. We need to get going."

Kelsey took off her diving tank and secured it to the dive tank holder. The rest of the crew scurried about trying to secure water samples and instruments when a large wave hit, knocking everyone off balance. As they were righting themselves from the first wave, a second crashed the deck and caught Carlos. He struggled to gain his footing and a hand-hold on the side of the boat, but he was overpowered. He disappeared over the side of the boat with the wave.

"Man overboard!" shouted Kelsey. Captain Makepeace grabbed the ship's wheel to bring the 25-foot vessel around. Carlos was bobbing off the starboard side.

"Hang on Carlos!" called Kelsey as she threw him a life ring and a line. Carlos grabbed it and held on. The storm was on top of them now. The boat pitched in the 15-foot waves as Kelsey and Evan, a student intern from the University of Florida, pulled Carlos close to the boat. The boat heaved in the waves. Lightning fractured the sky around them. Rain pounded as Kelsey and Evan dragged Carlos into the boat. The storm was raging. In the urgency of rescuing Carlos the crew had not noticed that the strap holding the dive tank had snapped and the tank was crashing back and forth across the beam of the boat. It hit the port side, then the starboard, then the port again making a subtle crack in the hull. As the waves and rain pounded the small craft from the exterior, so did the tank from the interior. The last thing Kelsey saw was a 30-foot wave crashing over the boat and its crew.

Word came from the Coast Guard search and rescue helicopter team: there was only debris at the site where Captain Makepeace had called "May Day. May Day." There were pieces of the splintered boat floating in the now-calm sea—a seat cushion, a ring bouy, part of the hull—but there was no sign of Captain Makepeace, nor Evan, nor Carlos, nor Snorkel's mom. They were deemed missing at sea and presumed dead.

Snorkel's grandpa, her mom's dad, was at the house with Sean, Snorkel and her Uncle Rob when the evening news confirmed the story. "Four marine biologists from NOAA were caught in a sudden storm this morning while they were measuring water quality off the coast of Key West. The "May Day" call came into the Coast Guard about 11 a.m. When Coast Guard helicopters arrived, there was no sign of the crew. The Coast Guard scoured the area off the marine sanctuary south and west of the Keys, but they found no evidence of the crew.

Among them was St. Augustine resident Kelsey McCorkle. All four are missing and presumed dead."

Uncle Rob, Sean's brother, quickly turned off the TV. A fearful silence filled the room. Grandpa muffled a sob and pulled out his handkerchief to wipe his eyes. Snorkel's dad stared at the blank TV. Uncle Rob gently put his hand on his brother's shoulder. The silence roared in Snorkel's head like a violent sea, but she didn't cry. She simply slipped from her dad's lap and went to her room.

She sat at her desk and stared at her map of world currents. She had looked at this map hundreds of times with her mom to calculate the distance travelled by the sea beans they had found on the beach. Seeds from tropical plants floated down rivers into the sea and into great currents of the world's oceans, and then onto the beaches. A small seed could travel 15,000 miles from one current to another, from Costa Rica to Nor-

way or the Canary Islands, or from Madagascar to Florida. Their travels made them magical.

(1) (Scan for link.)

Snorkel opened the drawer in her desk to a treasure of sea beans. She picked up a small gray sea pearl and heard her mother say, "In the Scottish Hebrides where your dad's family comes from, his grandmother used to wear sea pearls to ward off evil."

She picked up the pod of giant Entada beans. When she rattled it, she heard her mother say, "A lucky charm all the way from Madagascar." She was certain she saw her mom point to Madagascar on the map. "Oh and isn't this a lovely one from Costa Rica?" she heard as she saw her mom pick up a rare Mary's bean. "Imagine how magical it seemed when it got to Scotland." Snorkel traced the currents on the map from Costa Rica to Scotland. She heard her mom saying "All the expectant mothers

here held this one for an easy
birth. Maybe they were magic!
Maybe because they had come
from so far away. Maybe because
some actually had medicinal proper-
ties."

"The Norwegians made tea
from the sea heart husk. When sailors find one, they carry it for luck,"
her mom's voice said. Snorkel
could feel her mom slip the sea
heart necklace she had made for
her daughter over her head. Snorkel touched it and said, "I know
you are not dead."

(Scan for music.)

Sea Bean
Sung by
Katherine Archer

Drifting like a sea
bean,
on the currents of
the seas.
From the coral keys
of Florida,
to the volcanic
Canaries.

From the trees of
Costa Rica
to the beaches of South Wales,
the drifting little sea bean
has a sailor's salty tales.

'Round the ocean currents
a tiny pod can float.
The heart can then imagine
the safety of a boat.

Moving with the current
upon the ocean's swell,
A heart can then imagine
the seafarer is well.

CHORUS
Tiny sea bean ebb and flow.
Tiny sea bean where can you go?

Drifting like a sea bean
on the currents of the seas
from the straights of Madagascar
to the beaches of Belize

From the jungles of Guyana
to the ports of Newfoundland,
a tiny seed can travel
a distance that is grand.

REPEAT CHORUS

Through the Great Antilles
to a rough Norwegian Shore,
a heart can then imagine
a sailor home once more.

A tiny seed can travel
a distance that is grand
across a mighty ocean
to the place on which we stand.

REPEAT CHORUS

"No! Definitely not dead!" Snorkel reaffirmed as she looked at the map. She traced her finger over the site where her mom had been measuring water quality in the National Marine Sanctuary off Key West. She had gone there to protect the third largest coral reef in the world. She wasn't dead. She was drifting, like a sea bean. Yes. She was drifting on a piece of the boat or in a life raft. She was in the Florida Current passing by the Keys, and tomorrow she would be in the Gulf Stream. Snorkel used her nautical navigation map to measure the distance from Key West to St. Augustine: 424 nautical miles.

Snorkel knew that the Gulf Stream flowed at 4 nautical miles per hour or 96 nautical miles in 24 hours. Excitedly she measured 96 nautical miles with her compass and marked the distance on the map. Tomorrow morning her Mom would be near Miami. Next to the pencil mark, Snorkel wrote tomorrow's date, June 14. She swung the compass and marked off another 96

miles: Jonathan Dickinson State Park, June 15. Then Satellite Beach, June 16: Daytona Beach, June 17 at 11 a.m.: and St. Augustine the same day at 8 p.m. It would still be daylight. Drifting on the Gulf Stream, her Mom would reach St. Augustine in 4.4 days. She could be home in 3 more days!

Snorkel went to her closet and rummaged through the bottom. She found her mask, snorkel and fins and put them on. She would be ready.

She sat down on her bed. It had been a long day. She lay back on the pillow and fell asleep, knowing that her mom was safe, floating on the currents on her way back home.

In her dreams she saw her Mom sitting on the side of a rubber raft. Her hair was tied back with the sleeve of her shirt. She was gathering sea grass from the waves.

20

(1) Drift seed, Wikipedia, https://en.wikipedia.org/wiki/Drift_seed

Chapter 3:
Snorkel Builds a Sail

The morning after the Bucy brothers dunked Snorkel for the umpteenth time, she emerged from the house with only one small lock of hair missing from the duct tape episode. It didn't matter much. Her wild curls went in all directions anyway. She donned her life vest, then eased her kayak with its new outrigger into the canal. She slipped in and paddled off. Snorkel turned boldly onto the river and then held up at the Bucy's pier. The boys were not around. She waited a while then paddled toward the Vilano Pier. Suddenly, from nowhere, Brad and Brian came speeding to catch Snorkel. Brad went right. Brian went left. They circled and circled, but the outrigger held the kayak upright. Snorkel raised her fist in triumph. A woman in a kayak with a sail passed, giving Snorkel two thumbs up. It gave Snorkel an idea.

Snorkel flapped into the kitchen for lunch.

"Hey, Snork. How was your morning?" asked her dad.

"Snatched!" beamed Snorkel. Her dad winced from the slang.

"Language," he responded.

Snorkel didn't wait for him to ask why, but barreled into the story. "I went past the Bucy's pier, nice and slow." She sidled up to her dad, who was carrying lunch to the table. "I baited them to come at me. I was just past Larson's when they came outa nowhere!

ZOOM! Past me on the right!" Snorkel zipped past her dad on the right. "ZOOM! on the left!" Snorkel zipped around him on the left. "ZOOM! ZOOM! ZOOM! They went in circles, but they couldn't tip me!" Snorkel ran around her dad, who nearly dropped a plate of sandwiches. "My new outrigger is SNATCHED!"

"That's great, Snorkel. It was very brave of you to stand up to those bullies."

"You shoulda seen 'em. They just couldn't believe I was still upright."

"How about some lunch? Grilled cheese."

"Snatched!" Snorkel hopped onto the kitchen bar stool, as her dad winced again. "Dad?" Snorkel began taking a bite of sandwich.

"Mmmm."

"I was thinking, Dad. Could I get a sail for my kayak?"

"No. Absolutely not."

"But, Dad, I could go much faster with a sail than with my old paddle."

"That's just the point. The last thing I need is you speeding up and down the river, getting caught in a gust of wind and blown who knows where. It's enough to worry about you moving at kayak speed."

"But, Dad..."

"Nope! No! Unh un! Not happenin'! Not now. Not ever! Don't ask me again until you're 37!"

"Dad." Snorkel laughed and went back to her grilled cheese. She knew he would not change his mind, and she knew better than to persist. She also knew that she would come up with something.

~~~

From the dumpster in the alley behind the marina flew an old wooden Venetian blind, a piece of tattered sailcloth, some rope, a tent pole, some clamps and grommets. They clattered when they hit the ground. Snorkel muttered to herself as she landed next to her collection, "Hav'ta find someplace private to work on this." She knew the perfect spot. She stuffed the rope, the sail, cloth and the metalwork into her backpack. She gathered up the Vene, tian blind and tucked it under her arm. She would stop by the house to get one more item.

Her dad was on his cell and didn't notice Snorkel come in through the back door. She slipped up the stairs and into the bathroom. She climbed up on a small stool and removed every third snap hook from the shower curtain.

It was Saturday. No one would be at the elementary school. There was a sandy patch of ground just behind the playground that was surrounded on three sides by saw palmettos. She could work there without being seen. She dumped her materials on the ground and sorted them: pulleys, hooks, grommets, and coiled rop. Then she spread the sailcloth on the ground and smoothed it out. She pulled a neatly folded piece of paper from her backpack and laid it on the cloth. It was a pattern for a sail.

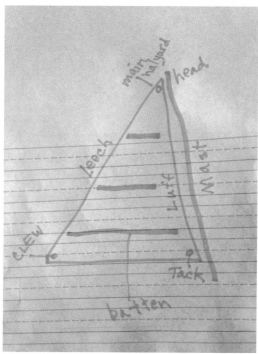

She hadn't expected it to take so long. It was getting close to sunset when she rolled up her new sail and secured it with bungee cords. She had carefully measured and cut the sail to the dimensions she needed, plus extra on the luff for a hem and grommets. She used slats from the

Venetian blinds to create battens. She punched a series of grommets into the luff (the part of the sail that is closest to the mast) and one in the head, (the top of the sail) for the halyard, the rope that pulls up the sail. She put another grommet each in the tack and clew (the corners at either end of the bottom of the sail). The shower curtain rings went in the grommet holes. They would slide the sail up the mast when Snorkel hauled it.

She had to hurry home for dinner or her dad would be worried.

Chapter 4:
Snorkel Meets a New Friend

Three dolphins cavorted in the canal behind Snorkel's house. She called out to them, "Good morning, Polly, Molly and Fred!" For all the world it sounded like high pitched whines from the dolphins, but Snorkel heard, "Good morning, Snorkel, beautiful day for a romp in the canal.

Snorkel carefully attached her new sail, still rolled up around the mast, to the velcro straps she sometimes used for a fishing pole. Then she put on her life vest and put the kayak in the water. She would wait until she got onto the river to try to attach the mast. She did not want her dad to see her latest invention. She knew he would not be pleased.

She was just past the Bucys' close to the riverbank. She looked up and down the river. They were nowhere in sight. That was lucky. She detached the mast and sail from the side of the kayak. She bunched up the sail so it wouldn't catch the wind, stood up and lifted the mast. She couldn't leave the mast permanently attached, so she Gorilla®-glued a piece of PVC pipe to the floor and front edge of the cockpit so she could take the mast down before she got near home. She was sliding the bottom of the mast into the PVC pipe when the Bucy brothers appeared on their jet skis coming from Vilano Beach. They zoomed past her on both sides.

"Take that you stupid, geek!" shouted Brad Bucy.

"Yeah," shouted his brother. "Stupid girl geek!"

The outrigger kept and Snorkel held her balance. She shook her fist and shouted back, "No wake. No wake. This is a no wake zone!"

Then the jet skiing brothers crossed behind her and began to circle her in opposite directions, one clockwise and the other counter-clockwise. The kayak rocked in the wakes. Snorkel slipped, lost her balance and with a big splash landed in the water.

She heard the brothers laughing and cheering as she surfaced. She was coughing and sputtering as the laughing boys zoomed away. That's when she heard a cry for help. She looked around, but didn't see anyone. Then she heard the cry again.

"Oh nooooooo! Not again. Oh noooooo. Please somebody help me!"

Snorkel twisted and turned in the water. She spun in a 360 but saw no one. "Hello," she called out, "Who's there?"

"I think I'm bleeding. I can't find my Lipzzz. Oh no, this can't be happening again!" cried the invisible voice.

"Where are you?" called Snorkel, nearly in a panic. "Are you hurt? I can't see you?"

"I'm right here, next to you," said the voice adamantly.

Snorkel jerked her head in the direction of the voice, but there was no one there. "Where?"

"I'm here. In the water!"

Snorkel ducked under the water. Luckily, she was wearing her mask and snorkel. There about four feet from her was a half-ton manatee, just next to her kayak.

"Can you help me?" blubbered the manatee.

"Of course!" said Snorkel, and she swam up to the manatee, careful not to touch her. They were face-to-face. The manatee was nearly hysterical.

"Am I bleeding? I can't even look to see if my Lipzzz is still there. It helps them find me. Oh dear. Oh dear. I hope nothing is missing."

"What would be missing?"

"Well the last time this happened, the propellers took off my right flipper." And the manatee rolled over in the water to show Shorkel where her flipper was missing. Snorkel looked politely and was horrified. There was just a stump with a large pucker where her flipper should be.

"Oh no!" Snorkel cried. "That's terrible. Does it hurt?"

"Not now. Can you see if I'm all in one piece? And if I have my Lipzzz?" Snorkel was looking right in the manatee's face directly at her lips. "Your lips?" she puzzled. "They seem just fine."

"No! My Lipzzz 347. It's around my paddle. It's a...a stalker."

"Oh." Snorkel swam around the frightened sea cow, still being careful not to touch her. Manatees are endangered. Snorkel knew touching one was not allowed. There was no bleeding. Nothing seemed missing, and

28

there was a tracking device tied around the manatee's tail. Snorkel examined it closely. It was marked "LPZ 347."

Snorkel swam around the other side of the manatee and looked her in the face.

"I didn't see any blood or any fresh gashes. But you do have a lot of old scars. There is a tracking device attached to your tail, er paddle."

"Thank goodness. My Lipzzz is still there!" That seemed to calm the frightened creature. Snorkel was curious. "Where did you get it?" she asked.

"Oh. At the Lily Pond Zoo. I was in rehab there for a few months after the speeding boat hit me in a no-wake zone," explained the manatee.

"That must have been horrible!" exclaimed Snorkel. "I hate it when they speed in a no-wake zone!"

The manatee continued. "I don't remember all of it. It could have been much worse. I have friends who've been hit by boats..." she paused and her eyes seemed to tear up "...who haven't made it." She sniffled. Then she told Snorkel the whole story of being found by the manatee rescue unit and gently lifted in a big swing out of the water and into a boat. "I never thought that I would be in a boat. I guess I passed out. When I woke up, the other manatees told me I was at the Lily Pond Zoo and had just come out of surgery."

Snorkel pulled herself out of the water back onto her kayak. "I know about the Lily Pond Zoo! My Uncle Rob works at Florida Wildlife Control. He's told me about manatees and boating accidents."

"Everyone was nice. I'm grateful they rescued me and saved me. It was comfortable there, but I like it a lot more swimming around the rivers and ocean."

Snorkel was so curious. She had about a million questions she wanted to ask the manatee. "How long since you were released?"

"Just a few weeks," replied the manatee. "I've been doing very well, but those jet skis were so close, and I didn't know which way to go. Noise can be very confusing underwater. Then I panicked. All I could think about was last time. And when I tried to swim away, my Lipzzz got sucked into the wake."

"That would have scared me, too." Snorkel tried to reassure the manatee. "Just a few weeks ago, my flipper, well it's not a real flipper, so it's not the same thing at all. But I use it for swimming." Snorkel's feet were hanging over the side of the kayak and she showed the manatee her old blue flipper and the new yellow one. Then Snorkel told the manatee her story.

"It was my birthday. Mom, Dad, Grandpa, Uncle Rob and his girlfriend Patty, Aunt Kisten and Uncle James and my cousins, Louie and Tanisha were all there in our backyard. Louie and Tanisha had made a big sign that hung between two palm trees. It said, 'Snorkel's Birthday Party.' My mom brought out the cake with 10 flaming candles. I wished I would always be that happy."

When she thought about her birthday now, sitting in the middle of the river talking with the manatee, she almost cried. But that was not the story she was telling. She was telling the manatee about her lost flipper.

"Well, anyway," said Snorkel. "My Grandpa gave me a big box with two beautiful new yellow flippers."

Snorkel loved the new yellow flippers. She had thrown her arms around her Grandpa. Her old blue flippers were faded and held together at the back with a piece of duct tape. She wanted to try the new ones right away, but it was too late to go to the beach. The next day, Snorkel rode her bicycle there, and tucked in the basket were her new yellow flippers.

Snorkel was so excited to try the yellow flippers that she ignored the first rule of the beach. Never turn your back to the water. Waves are powerful.

They can knock you down if you are not paying attention. For just a moment at the edge of the surf, Snorkel turned her back to the ocean to admire her new flippers in a shallow pool. In an instant, a big wave knocked her down and pulled her into the undertow. The riptide pulled her straight out to sea. As it did, it pulled one of her new flippers off her foot. In a heartbeat Snorkel was 300 yards from shore. Being a strong swimmer, she knew what to do to break free of the rip current. She swam parallel to the shore to-

ward the nearest breaking waves. She knew that they meant the end of the rip current. Then she swam diagonally toward the shore.

"Well," said Snorkel as she finished her story. "I had to swim a long way to get free of the riptide. I was pretty far up the beach when I got back. I was very lucky. It was scary. I didn't tell my mom, though. She would have killed me." Snorkel looked down at her mismatched flippers. "Now, I have one new yellow flipper and my old faded blue flipper."

The manatee looked at Snorkel intently. "That would have been scary. You must be a very good swimmer indeed."

31

Then it struck her. Maybe this fine swimmer could help her. It was such a grand idea that the manatee blurted it right out. "Since you're such a good swimmer, maybe you could help me find my lost flipper. Then I could take it back to the people at the zoo, and they could sew it back on."

"Oh. I don't know," gasped Snorkel. It seemed quite an unlikely idea.

"Oh, please, ah, oh...I don't even know your name. I'm Matilda." She extended her left flipper toward Snorkel.

"Pleased to meet you, Matilda. I'm Snorkel McCorkle," she said as she shook the manatee's remaining hand.

And that was how Snorkel McCorkle met Matilda the Manatee and they began their great adventure of the lost flipper.

Chapter 5:
Snorkel Tracks Her Mom

Snorkel's room was dark except for the light of the full moon shining in the open window. She slipped from her bed and tiptoed to her desk as quietly as she could wearing her flippers. She turned on the lamp. It added a small soft circle of light to the desktop and the chart of ocean currents on the wall behind.

She had been marking the distance her mom would have floated on the currents every night for the past three months. Pencil marks with dates ran up the East Coast to North Carolina and then out past Newfoundland into the North Atlantic Current, where they started to split off in three major directions: Northwest on the Irminger Current toward the tip of Green-

land and around Iceland, Northeast past Ireland and Scotland toward Norway on the Norwegian Current, and East and South on the Azores Current toward Spain, the great African continent and the Canary Islands.

At each point along the currents she marked, Snorkel pictured her mom and what she would be doing. Off the coast of St. Augustine she had imagined her, hair tied back with the sleeve of her shirt, dragging the rest of her shirt behind the rubber raft with the other sleeve knotted to catch minnows and sea grass. Snorkel saw seaweed drying on the side of the raft and plastic bottles in the rope lines around the sides of the raft to catch rainwater.

By the time Snorkel marked off

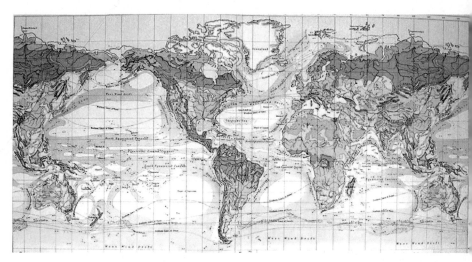

the raft's travel past North Carolina, she imagined her mom with dread-locks, the shirt turned into a makeshift cover with pieces of plastic stretched above a driftwood and ghost net frame with plastic bags funneling rainwater into plastic bottles. Snorkel saw micro-filament and ghost net trailing behind to catch fish.

When she marked off the turn to-ward the south on the Azores current, she saw her mom pulling up a plastic crate with crabs in it and squid drying in the ghost net added to the frame. She knew her mom was drifting on the currents just like the sea beans she

had taught Snorkel about. If a tiny seed could travel halfway around the world, Snorkel could believe her mom was landing on a distant shore.

Snorkel finished the last mark for the day. She pictured her mom in the Canary current. She could be moving toward the Canary Islands. In a few days she would be near Tenerife. Maybe she would drift toward the is-land and land. She imagined it would be beautiful there. She moved to the window to look at the moon. Snorkel said, "Good Night," to her mother and the moon and slipped back into bed.

Chapter 6:
Figaro
the Opera-Singing Pelican

After school, when Snorkel reached the pier, she looked for a trash can for the plastic debris she had picked up along the beach. She was dumping her canvas bag with its plastic bottle caps, straws, balloons, styrofoam, chunks of plastic crate, bits of building insulation, a plastic glove and half a dozen grocery bags when she heard Matilda. "Hey, Snorkel! Beautiful day!" said the manatee. "Yes, it is!" beamed Snorkel, excited to see her new friend.

"Have you got a couple of minutes?" asked Matilda. "Just a few," replied Snorkel. "I'm on my way home for supper."

"Oh. I wanted to introduce you to a friend of mine. There he is now! His name is Figaro. We're just in time for his act."

They heard his voice as he flew across the Vilano Beach peninsula, gliding above the Magic Beach Motel just as the neon was coming on and the bright pink flamingos were lighting the dusky sky.

He tilted to give a quick look toward Benedetto's Ristorante and the 180 Grill to see if anyone had dropped some pizza, then a quick buzz over Beaches to look for sweet potato fries before landing with a great flourish and flapping of wings on a post just beyond the Bluebird of Happiness. Snorkel turned to see a chubby pelican with head feathers dangling like a Timacuan and a mangled left foot balanced on the post. He continued to sing.

I'll sit on the deck
'Til that angler throws me
the last of her catch.
When my belly is full I'll
belch real loud,
Sit on the deck and
be part of the crowd.
Here come my friends.
The fun never ends.
This neighborhood
Is just like Hollywood.
This time of day,
the sun is just right.
The stage is set.
I'm ready for the spotlight.
I'll fluff up my feathers,
dance on the rail.
Singin' 'Smelly fish heads
an' tiny shrimp tails!'
With my belly full,
I'll belch real loud,
Pose on the deck
'til I gather a crowd.
Sing Pavarotti
'til I get their attention.
Then share with them all
my latest invention:
O solo mi o...
Smelly, smelly fish heads are best
Jelly, jelly fish give me indigestion!
Burrrrrrrrrrrrp!

"I'm flyin' in.
It's dinner time.
Here at the pier.
The food is so fine.
I just can't wait
I love that bait
Put on that pout
And hold it all in
my pouch.
I'll take my time, I LOVE to dine
A smorgasbord
Of all my favorite kinds:
A pepperoni pizza left on the rail.
Smelly fish heads and
Tiny shrimp tails.
An ice cream cone
a little boy dropped.
It all tastes so good I just can't stop.
Like a beggin' dog

Figaro's Theme
Sung by
Chris Carlson

36

Singing in a low bluesy voice, Figaro buzzed from place to place gobbling up the food and keeping it all in his pouch.

Figaro caught the ice cream cone before it hit the pier. The little boy didn't have time to cry, he was so captivated by the singing bird. Truth is, he had gathered quite a crowd of people cheering and clapping as he flitted about catching bait and fish heads in mid-air. He was quite the performer. Snorkel had heard about him before. Her Grandpa talked about seeing the Opera Singing Pelican when he was fishing at the pier, but Snorkel had never seen him. He was taking a final bow and the crowd was breaking up when Matilda called to him.

"Hey, Figaro." He turned toward her.

"Hey, Matilda. You catch my act?"

"You betcha. It was great!" Then she gestured toward Snorkel. "This is my friend Snorkel McCorkle. She's gonna help me find my lost flipper."

"Ah, Snorkel, did you say? That's quite an unusual name for a human girl. Pleased to meet you." Figaro bowed grandiosely to Snorkel.

"Pleased to meet you, too, Mr. Figaro!" smiled Snorkel.

"Just Figaro, please." He cocked his head.

"That was a great show, er... um...Figaro. My Grandpa told me about you. He fishes down here sometimes. He said there was an opera-singing pelican. I guess you are famous."

"Oh well." He blushed. His white body turned pink from his head to his chest. "Just around here at the pier. Two acts a day: breakfast and supper shows."

"Supper shows," repeated Snorkel. "I'd better get going, or I'll be late for mine. My dad'll worry. Nice meeting you, Figaro. Bye Matilda!" she called over her shoulder as she ran up the beach.

Chapter 7: Figaro Fends off the Bucy Boys

The next morning Snorkel walked to school by way of the beach. It was the long way, but she loved to be on the beach in the morning. She always left a half hour early so she could have extra time. There were dog walkers on the beach with their dogs, all of whom knew Snorkel. They raced up to her to say hello or lick her face. The yellow lab was Lucy. The feisty Pomeranean was Cappuccino, and the brindle cairn terrier was Zoro. There were fresh tide pools and a new line of wrack where she could look for shark's teeth and sea beans.

Snorkel flapped along the seaweed wrack line looking for treasure. In the tide pool was a rare hamburger bean Before she picked it up, she documented it with her camera.

It was nestled in a pile of seaweed along with a broken spork, a blue bottle cap, a feather, and some random bits of broken plastic. She stuffed the sea bean in her pocket and collected the trash in the reusable bag she kept in her backpack for just this purpose.

Just up the beach, Snorkel picked through a jumble of seaweed and found a shark's tooth and an antidote vine sea bean! That was a huge find. The antidote vine bean was probably from South or Central America. Its large shape fit nicely into the palm of her hand. Finding the sea beans reminded her of her mother. It gave her hope.

Snorkel was late for school. She had spent too much time sifting through the wrack. No one was left on the playground except the Bucy brothers and their psycho pal Henry. They blocked her way as she ran for the school entrance. Brad stepped forward directly onto Snorkel's flippers making it impossible for her to move. "Hey, fish face! What's your problem?" bellowed Brad directly into Snorkel's face.

Snorkel tried to break free, but just fell down. Brad leered at her. "You know what your problem is fish face? You need to take off that mask and snorkel and become just a geek girl again!" He reached for them, but Snorkel put her arms over her head and rolled. She broke free tripping Brad in the process. The other two boys surrounded her while Brad got up. As she scrambled to her feet, a loud squawk filled the air. They all looked up just as Figaro dumped a pouch full of canal water and fish on Brad's head. Sopping wet, Brad sputtered as Figaro hovered between him and Snorkel. His 12-foot wingspan was impressive.

The other boys laughed until he glared angrily at them. Then Brad spun toward Snorkel. "I'll get you for this fish face!" he promised as he and the other boys headed for the door. "Yup. I'll get you," he said, dripping water as he walked.

Henry laughed, "Who's fish face now?" as they walked away. Brad clapped him on the head.

"Are you okay, Snorkel?" Figaro asked.

"Yes, thanks, Figaro. What are you doing over here?"

"Well there's a small canal where the fishing is good and the playground has some of my favorite snacks—fruit rollups, chips, an occasional candy bar. I usually cruise by once a day or so."

"I'm so glad you were cruising by now. Thanks for helping me out."

"Anytime, Snorkel. You take care, okay?"

"Okay." The bell rang. "Gotta go. Thanks again, Figaro," said Snorkel as she raced through the door.

41

Chapter 8:
A Fight During Show and Tell

"What do you have to show us today, Mary Elizabeth?" asked her teacher Ms. Murray. Snorkel was standing with a small group of kids in her class sharing her sea bean find from the morning and her video of the tide pool.

Brad Bucy sneered at her and silently mouthed "Mary Elizabeth, fish face." Snorkel gave him a side-eye.

"Just come up and show everyone what you found," said Ms. Murray. Snorkel flapped to the corner of the room with the big map of the world. As she passed Brad, he hissed under his breath, "I will get you, geek!" Snorkel ignored him. She held up her treasure for the class.

"I found this hamburger bean this morning on the beach. It could have come from Africa. The plant it comes from is native to the rain forests of Africa, Central America and South America. The seeds get washed into rivers and out to sea. Then they are picked up by the currents." Snorkel pointed to the map as she continued. "The Canary Current comes along the east coast of Africa and joins up with the North Atlantic Equatorial Current. Then it moves across the Atlantic into the Antillies Current and hooks up with the Florida Current. The beans come around on the currents and wash up on beaches in Florida. They are easy to find, if you know what you're looking for."

"Thank you, Mary Elizabeth." said Ms. Murray. "Is that a different kind of sea bean you have around your neck?" Snorkel's hand went to the seaheart her mother had given her and clutched it. She choked a little when she answered. "This is a seaheart. Sailors think they're lucky because they are so rare. They wear them when they go out to sea." She paused for a moment to fight back some tears, then she continued, "This is the seaheart my mom gave me for good luck."

Brad blurted out a deep laugh, "Ha. Wasn't very lucky for her!"

Snorkel snapped around to look at him directly. "What did you say?"

"I said," answered Brad, "It wasn't very lucky for her!" That was more than Snorkel could bear. "Take it back!" she cried as she rushed at Brad and knocked him to the floor. Fists and fins and curls were flying as the two wrestled in a tangle in front of the entire class. Ms. Murray had

to pull Snorkel, arms still flailing, off a distraught-looking Brad.

~~~

The school hallway was empty as Snorkel and her dad walked silently toward the door. He opened it for her, and she stepped out into sunlight that was entirely too bright for her mood. Her head was down as they walked to the car.

Sean started, "Snorkel, you can't go around jumping on everyone who says mean things."

"But, Dad..."

"There's a zero tolerance of violence policy at school. And rightfully so."

"But, Dad. What he said was violent. And he..."

"You're suspended from school for the rest of the week."

"But what he said about Mom..."

"I don't care what he said. You are responsible for your actions."

They climbed into the car and buckled up. Her dad sat for a moment before he looked at her and said, "I have to work, Snorkel, and there's no one to look after you. I can't be worried about you getting into trouble and being alone at home." Snorkel just sat quietly as he started the car and they drove away.

~~~

That night Grandpa was there for supper. Snorkel was so happy to see him. She told him about her morning at the beach. Grandpa was from "The Islands," and he knew everything there was to know about the sea and the beach. He had taught her mom to swim and dive and fish. They both had taught her.

Snorkel rummaged around in her pocket for the hamburger bean. "Isn't it a beauty, Grandpa?" "It is a beauty, indeed," he agreed. "Where do you think it's from?" he asked. "I suspect Costa Rica," said Snorkel. "I suspect you are right," affirmed Grandpa. "See the 'smiley' at the base of the hamburger bun?" He

turned it to show her. "It's thin and upturned, different from the ones from Belize. I guess you got yourself a *Mucuna urnes.*"

Suddenly Snorkel's dad interrupted. "Grandpa, would you like some coffee?" His serious tone troubled Snorkel. "Sure, Sean. I would. Thanks." Her dad brought two cups of coffee to the table with a plate of cookies. Grandpa added milk and sugar and began to stir his coffee in the way only he did. It was a ritual. He put the spoon in the back of the cup, pulled it forward, lifted it straight out, moved it along the surface of the coffee without touching it, then put it down again at the back of the cup and did it again. If he were thinking about something, or worried, he could do this for minutes at a time. Snorkel thought he looked like a robot stirring coffee when he did that. Spoon in down the back of the cup, forward, up the front, across the top, in down the back, forward, up, across,

44

down, forward, up, across, down. He seemed especially lost in the motion tonight.

Snorkel's dad broke the silence. "Snorkel, you know we love you very much," he said. She braced herself for something horrible. "I know it's hard," he continued. "But you have to give up this idea that your mom is coming home. We are all devastated that she's gone, but we have to face the facts."

"She isn't dead, Dad. She isn't dead!" protested Snorkel. "I just know, she's drifting..."

"Mary Elizabeth," interrupted Grandpa, softly but seriously. "Everybody's been giving you time to come to this on your own. It's such a big thing to do. But it isn't healthy to let you keep going on pretending she's coming back. She's lost at sea, darling grandbaby, and she wouldn't want you to go on like this. Give us a hug good night and run up to bed. Your Papa will come up in a bit. For his sake, try, okay?"

Snorkel held back her tears and hugged her Grandpa and then her dad. She could barely look at them. She loved them dearly, but they were in such terrible denial.

~~~

Snorkel sat quietly, elbows on her desk, her head in her hands as she studied the current map. She imagined her mom, the ends of her beautiful dreads sun-bleached, as she checked the fishing nets trolling behind the raft. Seaweed and cuttlefish were drying in the net of her makeshift covering. Pulling in the net, Kelsey finds a gilt-headed seabream. Snorkel knew they are common to the Mediterranean Ocean and the Spanish and African Pacific coasts. To kill and fillet the fish, Kelsey uses the knife she's made of a sharp piece of plastic tied to a driftwood handle with fishing line. Snorkel leaned back from her daydream and smiled.

45

Chapter 9:
Suspended and Grounded

The next morning was Snorkel's first day of suspension. When her dad came down for breakfast, Snorkel was making banana pancakes. Batter dripped on the counter, the stove and the floor. Her dad was quiet about the mess. She was in enough trouble without adding this.

"I made your favorite pancakes." Snorkel beamed, handing him a plate of kid-made pancakes. If only she could get her dad to lighten up about the suspension, she might be able to spend the day at the beach. "And coffee!" The brew was dark and steamy. Sean noticed the grounds spilled on the counter and floor.

"That's nice, Snorkel," he said, accepting her offering. "But you are still grounded. You are not to leave the yard today. Grandpa will check on you at lunchtime."

Snorkel nodded trying to retain her earlier sunny mood, but her head sank to her chest. She watched silently as her dad finished his pancakes and gulped down his coffee. "If you have any problems call Grandpa or Uncle Rob, okay?" He kissed her on the top of her curly head. "Love you. I'll be home around six." Snorkel sighed. "Bye, Dad. Love you, too," she mumbled as he went out the back door.

Snorkel hung off the end of the dock. Only her head and arms were in the water, so she must officially still be in the yard, she reasoned. She had her camera trained on a school of fish when Matilda paddled into the shot.

"Hey, Snorkel! What are you doing?" asked Matilda. "Shouldn't you be in school?

Snorkel popped out of the water, because she couldn't talk underwater.

"I'm suspended," she told Matilda.

"Oh good," replied Matilda. "I'm suspended, too. It means like floating, right?"

"It means I can't go to school for the rest of the week," said Snorkel.

"That's great, isn't it?" answered Matilda. "We can suspend together!"

"No. It's bad. I punched a kid who said something mean about my mom."

"Well," responded Matilda. "He probably deserved it."

"He did! But now, besides being suspended, I'm also grounded," said Snorkel.

Matilda was confused. English is often confusing. "Suspended and grounded? Isn't that an oxymoron?" asked the gentle sea cow.

"Well, yes and no. They usually go together. It means I can't leave the yard," explained Snorkel.

"Just like the zoo," said Matilda. "So sorry, Snorkel."

Just then there was a huge splash right next to the dock. They looked around to see that Figaro had plunged into the canal and caught a fish. He swallowed it as he floated on the water nearby.

"Hey Snorkel," called Figaro. "Is this where you live?"

"Yup." she answered.

"Nice digs. The fishing is great over here. I come here often. Didn't know you lived here, but then I didn't know you, did I?" offered the pelican.

Suddenly a bubbling, rumbling sound came from the canal. Figaro flew straight up, covering his beak with one wing while keeping himself aloft by flapping the other one. "Run, Snorkel, run!" he screamed.

Snorkel tried to run backward up the bank from the dock, but tripped over her flippers and fell. She pinched her face and covered her nose. "What's that awful smell?" she gasped. "I've never smelled anything so nasty!"

"It's Matilda!" called Figaro from his safe distance.

"Matilda?" questioned Snorkel.

"Come on guys. It's not that bad," chimed in Matilda.

"No worse than usual. How do you do that? Whatever do you eat?" asked Figaro.

"If we could bottle that, we'd have the world's worst stink bomb. Think what would happen if I set it off in math class!" exclaimed Snorkel. She imagined setting one off under Brad Bucy's desk and everyone scattering while she laughed through her snorkel.

Figaro settled onto the dock next to Snorkel.

"Guys. Really. I can't help it. I'm just built this way," said Matilda trying to explain. "I was really hungry, so I ate about 40 pounds of sea grass. I have to eat 10 to 15 percent of my weight each day." She tried another tack; she sang.

"I'm bubbling along
From river to sea
I'm a grazing
bovine under water.
I'm gentle and calm
I live to sleep and eat.
It's how I'm designed
'Cause I'm a manatee.
I'm a half a ton of floating,
     bloating nibblin' machine.
I'm gonna eat it if it's in the
water, and it looks really green.
And just like a cow
that walks on the land,
when the methane starts bubblin'
better watch where you stand.
'Cause sea grass
gives me sea gas.
I like to rest my head
On that river bed.
In between my meals.
Depends on how I feel.
Take a little cat nap
in my underwater flat.
So grand to be me.
Yeah I'm a manatee!
I'm a half a ton of floating,
bloat-ing nibblin' machine.
Gonna eat it if it's in the water
and it looks real green.

Sea Gas
Sung by
Duffy Bishop

And just like a cow that walks on
   the land,
when the methane bubbles
watch where you stand.
'Cause sea grass
gives me sea gas.
Sea grass
Gives me sea gas.
When you're boating by be careful.

Please observe the no wake zone.
I may be dining or sleeping
'Cause this water is my home!
I might be resting my head
On that river bed.
In between my meals.
Depends on how I feel.
Taking a little cat nap
in my underwater flat.
So grand to be me.
Yeah I'm a manatee
I'm a half a ton of floating,
bloating nibblin' machine.
And sea grass
Gives me sea gas.
Yeah sea grass
Gives me sea gas!
Excuse me!

50

"Whoa!" shouted Figaro from high above the pier. "Ok, we get it. 'You're a half a ton of floatin', bloatin', nibblin' machine, and sea grass gives you sea gas.'"

The gas bubbled. "Frrrp. Frrrp. Frrrp. Frrrrrrrp."

Figaro made armpit farting sounds "Whrrrp. Whrrrp. Whrrrp. Whrrrrp." Snorkel made mouth farts. "Blzbbb. Blzbbb. Blzbbb. Blzbbbb."

The harmony was glorious. They all fell over laughing. They laughed and laughed and laughed until they could hardly breathe. It was a perfect morning.

Manatee Fart!

Sax by Fox Hillyer

Chapter 10:
Snorkel visits the "LPZ"

"Good morning, everyone!" beamed Uncle Rob as he came through the kitchen door.

"Good morning, Uncle Rob!" said Snorkel through a mouthful of cereal, happy and surprised to see him. "What are you doing here?"

"Want a cup of coffee?" asked Sean.

"That would be perfect," said Uncle Rob as he sat on a stool at the counter.

"Thanks for looking after Snorkel today," said her dad as he handed Uncle Rob a cup of coffee.

"My pleasure!" smiled Uncle Rob.

"She did pretty well on her own yesterday, but I have to work late tonight..."

"Always happy to help," interrupted Uncle Rob. "Besides I have to go to the Lily Pond Zoo, and I can't think of a better zoo companion than Snorkel."

"Really! Uncle Rob," interjected Snorkel, suddenly excited. "Are we really going to the Lily Pond?" Uncle Rob nodded. "That's fantastic!" she enthused. "I have a friend who was just in rehab there."

The brothers stared at her quizzically.

"Uh. There's this manatee I met."

Their eyes got bigger.

"Er....I mean there's a manatee, and she lost a flipper, and she has a tracking device," Snorkel managed to say.

"Did you see her nearby?" asked Uncle Rob.

"Yeah," said Snorkel relieved. "She was in the river when I first met...er...saw her. Then I saw her again yesterday, out back in the canal. I'd love to find out more about her."

"Sounds great," said Uncle Rob. "We'll have time to stop by the manatee critical care unit at Lily Pond and check it out."

Sean grabbed his lunch and coffee and kissed Snorkel on the head. "You never cease to amaze me, Snorkel. Thanks Rob," he said on his way out the door.

"You 'bout ready, Snorkel?" asked Uncle Rob.

"Yup. As soon as I get my camera," said Snorkel slurping the rest of the milk from her cereal bowl and putting it in the sink with some water.

~~~

Snorkel was so excited to go to the Lily Pond Zoo with her uncle that she quite forgot to ask why he was going. When they got to his truck, which was marked Florida Fish and Wildlife Conservation, Snorkel heard a strange mewling sound coming from a carrying crate strapped to the back seat. Closer inspection revealed a small gray kitten with dark spots and blue eyes.

Snorkel's eyes bugged. "OMG! Uncle Rob. Is that a panther kitten?" she exclaimed.

"It is, Snorkel. Someone in Clay County found him half-starved along a county road." Since Florida panthers are both endangered and elusive, they are rarely seen. If they are encountered they are protected. "The man who found him left him there for several days until he determined his mother wasn't coming back. Then the man called our office. We've been feeding him 'round the clock, but he needs to be with specialists who can help him survive and then be released back into the wild when he's ready. I'm taking him to the Lily Pond Vet Clinic where they can take good care of him." <u>(2)</u>

"Do you think I could hold him, Uncle Rob? I know he's endangered, and shouldn't be handled. But he's so small, and I feel so sad for him to have lost his mama." Looking at Snorkel's small worried face, he said, "I think it would be okay this time, Snorkel." A tear ran down her cheek as her uncle gently placed the baby panther in Snorkel's arms. It was the first time he had seen Snorkel cry since her mother had gone missing.

By the time she and Uncle Rob got to the Manatee Center, Snorkel had made videos of the panther kitten, an injured flamingo, a newborn

orangutan and her mom, and three endangered African penguin chicks.

~~~

Dr. Gwen met Snorkel and Uncle Rob at the Manatee Center. "Is there anything in particular you would like to see?" asked the Doctor.

"Erm...well a friend of mine, er...a manatee...well a manatee I know was here recently," stammered Snorkel.

Dr. Gwen nodded and asked, "Why was she here?"

"Oh...ah, she lost her right flipper in a boating accident. She has a tracking device. I wondered if I could see where the veterinarians work on rescued manatees?"

"Sure," said Dr. Gwen. "Let's go by the surgery first. Then we can go to the recovery pool and tracking room."

In the surgery, veterinarians bent over a manatee stitching up several wounds on her back. Snorkel pulled out her camera to make a video.

"This manatee was lucky," said Dr. Gwen. "She has some nasty gashes along her back, but they're not too deep. She'll recover nicely. Boats are the biggest problems for manatees. Thirty percent of manatee deaths are because of boats. Manatees stay in relatively shallow water, maybe 3 to 6 feet deep, to eat the sea grasses and rest along the beds. They are no match for large boats with big propellers plowing through shallow water at high speeds."

Snorkel made a video of the vet working on the manatee. Dr. Gwen pointed out where its lungs were and how close they were to the gash. "Their lungs are pretty close to the surface of the back, near the spine. A propeller can puncture a lung and then the manatee drowns."(3)

Snorkel moved the camera toward Dr. Gwen. "If you ever see a manatee listing in the water, which means floating low on one side, her lung is probably punctured. Call Florida Fish and Wildlife Conservation Commission or us right away."

They moved to another wounded manatee. "The other danger," Dr. Gwen continued, "is monofilament and crab traps. This manatee caught her flipper in a crab trap. If she hadn't been able to get to the surface, she would have drowned. As it was, the circulation to her flipper was cut off. We'll have to remove it."

"That's what happened to Matilda, er my friend..... er the manatee I know," stammered Snorkel.

"She lost her flipper when the boat hit her. Can you reattach a flipper if it's cut off by a boat?"

"It would have to be immediately after the accident, and likely still partially attached to save it. The chances would not be good. Here's this manatee's x-ray."

"Wow!" cried Snorkel. "The bones look like a human's. There's an elbow and fingers!" ([4])

"That's right, Snorkel. Manatees have super flippers. They have bones similar to human fingers. If you look closely, you can see she has fingernails that help her walk on the bottom of the river."

"Could a manatee get a new flipper...like a mechanical one?" asked Snorkel.

"A prosthetic flipper? Hmm. Well, no one has done that yet, but they have given a dolphin a prosthetic tail. And some veterinarians have made special prosthetic limbs for land animals, so it might be possible," answered Dr. Gwen. "Let me show you this," she continued and played a video of dolphins and turtles and whales caught in ghost nets and fishing lines. "There's so much fishing line just floating in the water and old fishing nets that get tangled and cut free. They are just floating there like ghosts to trap marine mammals and fish."

"That must be what happened to Figaro." exclaimed Snorkel.

"Who is Figaro?" asked Dr. Gwen.

"He's a friend of Matilda's," blurted Snorkel until she saw the strange looks on Dr. Gwen's and her Uncle's faces. "Er, um, he's a pelican who hangs at the pier. He has a mangled leg. But he can still fly." She couldn't very well tell them that he could dance and sing and that he was the one who had helped her fight off the Bucy brothers two days ago before she got in the fight.

"He's a lucky one," offered Dr. Gwen. "Over a million sea birds and 100,000 marine mammals die each year from entanglement in nets, lines, traps and litter." (5)

Snorkel gasped at the numbers. "That's horrible! What can I do about it?"

"Well," said Dr. Gwen thoughtfully, happy that Snorkel wanted to help. (6) "You can make certain never to leave any fishing line in the water. Take it with you, or cut it into small pieces and recycle it. You can help teach others what to do with

their fishing line. And you can volunteer to pick up discarded line along the beach."

"Maybe we could put some signs up at the pier," said Snorkel.

"That's a great idea, Snokel," said Uncle Rob as they left the surgery and headed to the marine mammal tracking station.

(2) "Rescued Florida Panther Kitten Arrives at Lowry Park Zoo," Tampa Bay Times, February 20, 2014
https://www.tampabay.com/things-to-do/travel/florida/rescued-flori da-panther-kitten-arrives-at-lowry-park-zoo/2166519/

(3) The Florida Manatee, Florida Fish and Wildlife Conservation Commission
http://manatipr.org/wp-content/uploads/2014/08/SMC-Manat

 (4) Save the Manatee FAQ
https://www.savethemanatee.org/manatees/manatee-faq/

(5) "These Creepy 'Ghost Nets' Are Killing Thousands Of Animals Every Year," Elizabeth Claire Alberts, the dodo, March 19, 2018
https://www.thedodo.com/in-the-wild/ocean-animals-dying-in-l ost-fishing-gear

 (6) "Manage Your Fishing Line," Save Costal Wildlife
https://www.savecoastalwildlife.org/managing-fishing-line-waste

Chapter 11: Snorkel Downloads Matilda's Tracking App

In the tracking station were several screens with maps sporting blinking points of light, some moving and some stationary. One was labeled "turtles," another "dolphins," another "manatees."

"This is where we track the movements of the animals we release back into the ocean. We can see how far they've gone and where they travel every day. Do you know the number of the tracking device for the manatee you've seen?" Dr. Gwen asked Snorkel.

"Yes," replied Snorkel. "It's lip-zzz...er LPZ 347."

Dr. Gwen looked at the manatee screen to find it. " 347, 347...ah, here she is," Dr. Gwen pointed to a small red dot on the map. "If you follow her trail backwards," she said, showing Snorkel the dotted line behind the dot then tracing it back, "you can see where she's been. We released her back into St. Augustine inlet about two months ago. You can see where she's gone since. It seems she stays in the rivers mostly—the Mantanzas and the Tolomoto. She sometimes goes past the pier, through the inlet to the Atlantic."

"Wow!" said Snorkel.

"Here she is today in a canal," said Dr. Gwen.

"Snorkel! That's the canal behind your house. Is that where you saw her?" exclaimed Uncle Rob.

"Yes!" said Snorkel excitedly. "She must be looking for me. I told her I was grounded."

The adults gave Snorkel another strange look.

"Er...I see her there often...and in the river. Once I saw her down by the pier," she said, trying to smooth things over.

"You can track her on your phone if you download our app. It will ping if she moves in any unusual direction."

"Let's try it," said Uncle Rob pulling out his phone. He fumbled with it looking for the app. Snorkel got out her phone and showed him how.

"Er, thanks, Snorkel," he said rather embarrassed.

"Wow! It's working," shouted Snorkel holding up her phone. "You can see her moving back out towards the river!" Snorkel threw her arms around Dr. Gwen. "Oh thank you, Dr. Gwen. This is the best ever."

As they left the animal hospital area, they walked past the pools where the recovering marine animals are kept until they can be returned to the water. Volunteers were bottle feeding the orphaned manatee calves.

"Manatee calves stay with their mothers for at least two years," explained Dr. Gwen. "A lot of calves here were orphaned or separated by boats. We keep them here until they are able to forage and go out on their own."

Snorkel thought that the little calves' faces were just as wrinkly as Matilda's.

"They have to weigh 600 pounds before we can release them," continued Dr. Gwen.

"Do you have any more information about Matilda, er manatee #347?" asked Snorkel.

"Let me see," said Dr. Gwen, looking at the tablet she was carrying. "It says that manatee #347 weighed 1216 pounds when she was released."

"That's half a ton!" cried Snorkel before belting out, "She's a half a ton of floatin' bloatin' nibblin' machine," from Matilda's song.

Uncle Rob shot Dr. Gwen a look as if to say, "I know she's a little unusual." The scientist nodded in acknowledgment.

Chapter 12:
Three Steps Forward,
One Step Back

The next morning was Saturday, and Snorkel was super excited to tell Matilda about her day at the Lily Pond Zoo. She looked at her phone and raced down the stairs as fast as possible in her flippers. Her red curls bounced behind her. Matilda was hanging out by the dock.

"Hey Snorkel," Matilda called out when she saw her friend running toward her. "How was your trip to Lily Pond?"

"Awesome!" answered Snorkel. "I saw where you had your surgery and the rehab pool. I also saw you on the tracking screen...the place they track your Lipzzz. We downloaded an app to find out where you are. It's snatched!"

"You mean you can see me?" asked Matilda.

Snorkel pulled out her phone. "I can't see you," replied Snorkel, showing her friend the screen. "But I can see where you are. Your Lipzzz sends a signal. Look ... that little red dot beeping on the screen is you."

Matilda looked at the screen. "Oh my! I guess that's good."

"It's very good," declared Snorkel. "They can see where you are, and they learn a lot about manatee habits, too. Like where you go and how far you travel."

Suddenly Snorkel's smile disappeared and she looked sad. "What's the matter, Snorkel?" asked her friend.

"I wish my mom had a Lipzzz," she said forlornly. She sat for a moment quietly, then said, "I know that everyone thinks she's dead. My dad and Uncle Rob and Grandpa. They think no one survived the storm, and that the boat sank off the Keys. But I believe it got pulled out into the current. Maybe they got the life raft. They could have been pulled along the Florida current into the Gulf Stream. Then they could have been carried anywhere in the world. They could be drifting around like sea beans."

Snorkel seemed renewed for a moment. Then her spirits sank again. She turned to her friend, who was listening intently, and confided, "I can't really tell any of them what I think, because they think I'm not accepting reality. But

I know my Mom could have survived. I've plotted it out."

It was clear Matilda had been thinking seriously about Snorkel's story. "That thing you call the Gulf Stream," she asked, "is it like a warm river in the ocean?"

"Yes," answered Snorkel.

"I know that river...um stream," said Matilda. "Manatees follow it in the summer to go to the cold country. Sometimes we go pretty far away from here. We travel faster in the warm river, but we come back here in the cold season." And then she said something astonishing. "I know your Mom could float a long way on the warm river. I've heard manatees say that it goes to the other side of the ocean."

Snorkel could not believe her ears. "Oh Matilda!" cried Snorkel. For the first time she felt understood. "You're the only one who understands. You're my best friend."

Snorkel told Matilda all about tracking her mom on her ocean charts, a little like the Lily Pond people were tracking Matilda. She told her how she imagined her Mom in the lifeboat, with fishing net trawling behind and a plastic sheet and bucket she found for catching rainwater. By now her dreads would be tinged with blonde from the sun.

"She could catch fish and rainwater and eat sea grass," bubbled Snorkel. "My mom is so smart. She would know what to do. And maybe, if she got to Newfoundland or Ireland or Norway and landed on a rocky shore....Well maybe she has amnesia. Maybe she doesn't remember who she is, or us." Snorkel began to cry—a soft, nearly silent sobbing that moved her small shoulders up and down. Matilda could feel that pain and sadness in her own heart. She wanted so much to help her little friend.

"It's okay, Snorkel," said Matilda, trying to comfort her. "It must be so hard to lose your mother before it's time. I've learned that sometimes we have to go backward to go forward." She paused, then said, "Like when you tack when you're sailing. You can't always go in a straight line."

Matildia swam along the canal motioning for the girl to follow.

Matilda confided, "We manatees have a song that helps; it goes like this:

Three Steps
Forward
Sung by
Duffy Bishop

"Three steps for-
ward
One step back.
Sometimes it's
necessary
To retrace your
tracks.
While where you are
going
Matters the most
Knowing where you came from
Helps you not get lost.
I've got some scars on my back
And some go far beneath the
skin
I took a big breath, and I dove a
little deeper
'Till I found my joy, within.
Life's an ocean
That ebbs and flows
With sunny clouds above
And perils down below.
But there'll be islands
And coral reefs
Harbors to rest your heart
If you hold your beliefs.
I've got some pain in my past
It's part of who I am today

Made adjustments to my mast
And I've chosen my own way
Raise the jib or the spinnaker
now
Hang on tight to the mainstay
Got a good breeze, just the right
amount
Gently blowing us forward all
day.
Two steps forward
One step back
Sometimes it's necessary
To retrace your tracks
While where you are going
Matters the most
Knowing where you came from
Helps you not get lost."

The two friends swam and sailed to the music in their hearts all afternoon. Snorkel remembered Matilda's kind words. Suddenly Snorkel stopped and looked at her friend. "I'll do it," she exclaimed. "What?" asked Matilda.

"I'll help you get your flipper back. No matter what they said about it being impossible!" said Snorkel.

"Really? Snork, really?" Matilda shouted gleefully. "That's the best news in the world. And you're my best friend ever!" And the two friends grinned at each other as they had never grinned before.

Chapter 13:
A Sudden Storm

In their joyousness, the friends had not noticed the black clouds drifting over the estuary. A sudden gust of wind grabbed Snorkel's sail. It caught her off guard and yanked her kayak toward the pier and around the bend to the mouth of the Manzantas River. She grappled with the sail but couldn't get it down. One of the shower curtain rings she had used as a sail slug was hung up on the masthead block, and she couldn't bring it down. It was all she could do to hang on to the mainsheet and keep the kayak righted. Matilda kept close to the kayak in the water.

"Hang on, Snorkel. Just hang on. It will blow over soon. I'll be right with you." Snorkel could barely hear her over the howling wind. The wind had the little sail. The kayak and Snorkel barreled past the pier. Lightning flashed. Thunder roared. The wind pulled the mainsheet, the rope which controls the sail, from Snorkel's hand. The sail, the kayak and Snorkel were completely at the mercy of the storm. She struggled to retrieve the mainsail as the kayak passed the pier. Everyone there had fled to safety. Only Figaro saw the girl in the kayak headed toward the ocean. Spreading his twelve-foot wings, he soared after her.

Figaro dove at the mainsail sheet and caught it in his beak. He swooped over it to Snorkel, who clutched it tightly. Then Figaro turned toward the top of the mast to try to release the sail. He pulled at the curtain ring with his beak, but could not budge it. He tried to shout over the storm. "It won't budge, Snorkel. We'll have to ride it out." But the storm muffled his voice. He perched on the outrigger near Snorkel to give the kayak some weight. "Maybe all that pizza I ate will help out a little," he said.

"Thank you Figaro," called Snorkel above the storm. A wave crashed over the kayak. Snorkel held tightly to the mainsheet. The kayak with the bird and the girl bounced wildly over the incoming waves. They were headed straight out to sea.

~~~

Sean ran from his car to the house through the storm. "Snorkel!" he called from the kitchen, shaking off the water. "I'm home." There was no answer. He called up the stairs. "Snorkel? Are you up there?" There was no answer. He climbed the stairs and knocked on Snorkel's bedroom door. No answer. He opened the door, "Snorkel?" She wasn't there.

Sean ran down to the back yard and looked under the bougainvilla bush for Snorkel's kayak. It wasn't there. Rain was pouring down. He ran to the dock, where the boat was rocking in the storm, but there was no kayak. Sean scanned the canal. "Snorkel? Snorkel? Can you hear me? Where are you?" he called into the storm. He pulled his cell phone from his pocket. He heard Snorkel's voicemail. "Snorkel here. Leave a message." "Snorkel. It's Dad. Call me as soon as you get this message."

A lightning bolt lit the sky. He untied the small outboard motor boat, shoved it from the dock and jumped in. He steered the boat slowly along the canal toward the river looking and calling for Snorkel. The storm grew stronger. Rain lashed his face. Snorkel was not along the canal. As he turned into the river toward the pier, he rang his brother, "Snorkel is missing," he shouted against the wind. "Her kayak is gone. I think she's out in the storm." "Where are you?" asked Uncle Rob. "I'm in the boat going south on the river nearing the pier," Sean replied. "It's dangerous in that little boat. Snorkel's smart about weather. She's probably tied up at a friend's. Go back to the house. I'll meet you there." Uncle Rob hung up.

~~~

The storm raged over the kayak, Snorkel and Figaro. They barely managed to hang on, Snorkel with both hands and Figaro with his good foot, as rough seas tossed the small craft like a toy in the waves. The wind shredded the sail. Then it caught the mast, lifting and twisting it and flinging it toward Snorkel. The mast struck her on the head and knocked her into the churning water. Matilda came up underneath, trying to push her back into the boat. Figaro grabbed the belt on her life vest. Together they struggled to pull Snorkel back onto the kayak. Everytime the bird and manatee were close, the kayak crested a gigantic wave and fell into a trough, leaving Snorkel bobbing in the water, unconscious.

"You push from behind and let me try getting her leg. Maybe I can get a better grip," cried Figaro. The big bird seemed to swallow Snorkel's entire leg, but it gave him more leverage than the strap on the life vest. Against all odds they pushed and pulled the unconscious girl back into the kayak.

Figaro flapped his wing at her. "Snorkel! Snorkel! Can you hear me?"

"Is she breathing?" called Matilda. Figaro put his head to Snorkel's mouth. A puff of air ruffled his feathers.

"Yes!" Figaro cried gleefully. "She's still breathing. Stay close. I'll try to keep her warm." The large white pelican hunkered down and spread his wings over Snorkel to cover her, just as a huge wave rose high above and crashed over the bird, the girl and the kayak.

~~~

The sea surged. A huge wave rose. Lightning flashed. For a fleeting moment the outline of a woman huddled in a rubber raft appeared against the storm. Then the wave crashed and everything went dark. There was only the sound of the raging storm.

~~~

Flashing lightning lit up the entire harbor. Boats rocked and pulled violently against their ties. Officer Martin stood in the Coast Guard office looking at the wind ripping against the boats in the harbor. With him were Snorkel's dad and her Uncle Rob. "I'm sorry," said Officer Martin. "But the storm is too bad to send a search and rescue team now. We'll have to wait until it lets up. But we'll get someone out as soon as it's possible." The three men stood silently and looked out the window as a yacht broke free of its mooring and crashed up against the dock, ripping a hole near its bow. How much damage could it be doing to a tiny kayak and its small passenger?

~~~

The storm raged. Figaro clamped his good foot onto the side of the kayak as he covered Snorkel. Matilda braced the kayak with her half-ton body. The sea rose and fell in great waves and troughs, tossing the trio violently. Together, the bird and the manatee struggled to keep the little girl's limp body in the kayak.

Chapter 14:
Stranded in an Island
of Plastic

The sun rose brilliantly over a calm ocean. Figaro sat on the bow of the kayak with Matilda in the water alongside and Snorkel sleeping in the cockpit. Snorkel stirred. Figaro croaked. Snorkel woke up, yawning and stretching.

"Woohoo! You're awake! Matilda, Snorkel's awake!" shouted Figaro, flapping his wings and flying in a circle above the kayak.

"Where are we?" asked Snorkel.

"Hallelujah!" cried Matilda. "We thought we'd lost you. The mast gave you a rather nasty conk on the noggin' and you landed in the drink. We had a whale of a time trying to get you back in. Figaro guarded you all night!"

Figaro settled back down on the bow.

"All night? You mean it's Sunday?" asked Snorkel.

"Well, I wouldn't know Sunday unless it was a sea grass," said Matilda. "But the sun went down while you were out and the sun came up again before you were awake."

"Well where are we?" Snorkel asked.

Figaro flew up high above the kayak and looked for the shore. "We're really far out. I can't see the shoreline or the pier. But I know home is ..." He flung around

360 degrees with his wing extended and pointed where they needed to go. "In that direction."

Snorkel looked around at the damage. Most of the sail and mast were missing. The outrigger was mangled. She still had a paddle and her backpack. She gathered up the bits of the sail, mast and outrigger and attached them to the side of the kayak. "I can't leave this trash. Looks like I'll have to paddle back."

"Snorkel, have you got anything to eat?" asked Matilda. Rummaging through her backpack, Snorkel pulled out her waterlogged phone. "Guess I can't phone home." She dug through it some more. "I've got an apple and a protein bar. Maybe I can dry this out," she said, laying a very soggy peanut butter and jelly sandwich on the hull of the kayak. "Or maybe you want it Figaro?"

"Never turn down a good PB'n'J, Snork. But it might take us a while to get back. Better try to dry it out. It could always be bait." He turned, headed straight up into the air then dove into the water just off to the side of the kayak. He came up with several small fish sputtering in his bill. Tilting his head, he swallowed them down in one gulp.

"Plenty of good fish out here, though," he said. "Besides we're in this big island of sea grass. It's chock full of food." He dove into the water again and brought up a pouchful, which he dumped onto the kayak. "Try some of this." He started to eat a piece when Snorkel stopped him.

"Figaro! Stop!" shouted Snorkel. "You can't eat that. It's plastic."

With that warning, Figaro burped up a plastic toy soldier. It landed right in the middle of the pile of trash—red and white soda caps, small straws, bits of Styrofoam, part of a plastic bag, a piece of blue netting, a doll's arm, a broken plastic fork, a popped balloon still tied to its string and smaller pieces of brightly colored plastic.

"This is awful!" moaned Snorkel. She finally took a moment to look closely at her surroundings. It was a soup of plastic and other debris floating in the sea of grass. "We learned about this floating garbage in school, but it's worse than I imagined." (7)

"Yeah!" echoed Figaro. "Especially since it looks like food!"

The three friends looked at the plastic trash in the seagrass. Snorkel pulled a plastic bottle and a broken doll's head out of the garbage patch. Then she got excited and rummaged through her backpack. She pulled out her Go-Pro.

"We can't take all this back, but I can record it!" Snorkel made a 360-degree pan of the entire patch. It stretched as far as she could see. Then she made close ups of the plastic: tangled net, a broken milk carton, water bottles, a glove, and plastic bags hanging everywhere like upside-down clouds. Suddenly, through her lens, Snorkel saw a small sea creature caught in some ghost net.

"Oh no. There's a baby sea turtle!" She paddled closer to it. She didn't want to frighten it, but it was tangled pretty badly. "Excuse me, little turtle," said Snorkel.

"Yes?" replied the turtle.

"You seem to be in some trouble," said Snorkel. "Can I help you at all?"

"Yes, thank you. I think I'm caught," said the turtle. "I can't move forward, and I can't dive."

"Do you mind if I pick you up?" asked Snorkel. She was always mindful of doing something to an animal without their permission.

"If it will help," replied the turtle.

"I'll be very careful," said Snorkel. Cautiously, she reached into the water and lifted the little turtle onto the kayak. The blue plastic netting was twisted tightly around its head and front flipper. Snorkel pondered the situation. "I think I can unwind the netting from your flipper first and that should loosen it some around your head. Then we can take that off." Carefully Snorkel undid the netting that was catching the flipper. It loosened the netting around the turtle's head, but it had to be removed layer by layer. In trying to swim through the netting, the turtle had caught his head in several different loops. Snorkel worked to loosen and remove the first loop, then then second and then the third. Finally, the little turtle was free.

"Wow! Thanks! I can move my flipper and my head. I thought I was a goner," he exclaimed.

"Happy to help. I'm Snorkel, by the way, and these are my friends, Figaro and Matilda."

"How d'ya do," bowed Figaro.

"Hi!" said Matilda.

"My friends call me Riddles. And I'm very happy to meet you all. I was in a real mess."

"You're a Kemp's Ridley (8) aren't you?" asked Snorkel.

"Yes I am," replied Riddles.

"Where are you going out here all by yourself?" she asked.

"Well, I wasn't by myself," Riddles paused, "But I kinda got held up in the netting. And, well, um, my hatch mates had to go on without me."

"I'm sorry to hear that," said Snorkel.

"Well, I might be able to catch up now, thanks to you. You see, when we're just hatched there are hundreds of us. We all follow the moon across the big sand to the water. Some of us are lost then," explained Riddles.

"I learned about that," replied Snorkel. "Sometimes there are lights on the road or on houses and the baby turtles go the wrong way."

"Yes," said Riddles, "a lot of young turtles get confused and go the wrong way. When we get to the water, we swim and swim until we find the big grass. Then we land out here and float around and sun and play and eat. We learn how to take care of ourselves until we're big enough to go back to our hatching ground to lay our own eggs."

"Kind of like school," said Snorkel.

"It used to be a great place to grow up. Lots to eat. Lots of friends and places to hide from predators," reminisced Riddles. "But now it's full of danger. Oh well, it's the only home I have."

Snorkel thought of all the photographs she had seen of animals caught in debris—a turtle in a six-pack ring, a fish trapped in a plastic bag, seals caught in netting. Even massive animals like whales got caught in ghost netting.

"I'm so sorry that my species is so neglectful," Snorkel said to Riddles, "I promise to do something about this as soon as I get home."

"Well, thanks, Snorkel, for your help today. I guess I'd better get going."
With that Riddles dove off the kayak back into the swirl of grass and plastic.

"Nice meeting you, Riddles. Be careful," called Snorkel.

"Bye," said Matilda. "Be safe out there," said Figaro.

"Bye." called Riddles, and he disappeared into the swirl.

Suddenly Snorkel was agitated. "We have to do something about this!" she exclaimed. She picked up her camera and jumped into the water, much to the consternation of her aquatic pals. "Snorkel. No!" yelled Matilda.

"What are you doing?" cried Figaro. "We had so much trouble fishing you out!" Snorkel dove just under the water and began to shoot the mess of floating debris above, below and around her in the water. It was worse than a junkyard. There were all kinds of unimaginable bits of trash, both whole and broken.

She surfaced next to the kayak and pulled herself back in. She was visibly sad. "Who'd have thought," she said, "in the middle of nowhere, in the middle of the sea...Everything we've thrown away would be killing you and me."

Figaro was sad, too. He grabbed Snorkel's camera from the kayak and flew up to make an aerial shot of the gyre. There was plastic in every direction as far as he could see.

Snorkel's tiny voice continued.

It's a great big world.
Filled with endless wonders,
But I wonder why we can't end this tendency,
To take whatever we want
Discard and plunder
With no regard for the legacy we leave
Who'd have thought in the middle of nowhere,
Somewhere in our seas
Everything we've thrown away is killing you and me.

CHORUS
There's a heartbreak in the middle of the ocean,
stretching as far as the eye can see,

Heartbreak
Sung by Katherine

heartbreak in the middle of the ocean
filled with what someone threw out one
day,
Thinking it would all just go away.
But it's a cumulative effect.
One we will regret.

It's a deep deep sea
Thousands of fathoms
But I just can't fathom
How we cannot see
All the damage we've done
Will continue on.
Is this the way
We want to write history?
Who'd have thought in the middle of
nowhere
Somewhere in our seas.
Everything we've thrown away is kill-
ing you and me.

CHORUS
There's a heartbreak in the middle of
the ocean,
stretching as far as the eye can see,
heartbreak in the middle of the ocean
filled with what someone threw out one
day,
Thinking it would all just go away.
But it's a cumulative effect.
One we will regret.

Snorkel's voice drifted off as she sat in her kayak looking over the vast vista of swirling debris. Then Matilda broke the silence. "I know this is important, Snorkel. It hurts all the creatures of the land and sea. But to do anything, we have to get back. I mean we've got plenty to eat, but you've hardly got enough for breakfast."

Figaro flew back up to survey the situation. He still couldn't see land. "We've got a long way to go, gang. That way," he pointed. Snorkel put her paddle in the water and they started toward shore.

They had only gone a little ways when Snorkel's paddle struck something unexpected, a yellow flipper. "Wow! What's this?" she cried. She reached out to pick it up then tried it on. "Don't know if it's the one I lost, but it fits!" She was excited until she saw Matilda's face. "Sorry. I'm sorry, Matilda. I know we were looking for your flipper."

"Never mind, Snorkel," said the mild-mannered manatee. "We'll worry about that after we make it home." She gave Figaro a knowing glance. It may have been a good adventure for Snorkel so far, but Matilda and Figaro knew that there was a long way to go, and they might face much more danger before they reached shore. The tiny kayak and its bedraggled crew were in the midst of a vast bed of seagrass and plastic with only ocean beyond and no land in sight.

(7) NOAA, Marine Debris Program
https://marinedebris.noaa.gov/info/patch.html

(8) NOAA Fisheries, Kemp's Ridley Turtle, Overview
https://www.fisheries.noaa.gov/species/kemps-ridley-turtle

Chapter 15:
A Search in St. Augustine

Back in St. Augustine, the morning news was on. "In a distressing turn of events this morning," began the anchorwoman, "a 10-year-old girl, Mary Elizabeth McCorkle, is missing following last night's storm. She is believed to be in a kayak." Snorkel's school picture, showing her without her mask and snorkel, appeared as a chroma key behind the anchor. Brad Bucy spit his Froot Loops across the table. "Look!" he exclaimed. "It's Fish Face. She's missing."

The anchor was still talking. "Ironically," she continued, "The missing girl is the daughter of Kelsey McCorkle, one of the marine biology team that went missing three months ago while gathering water samples off the Keys." The picture of Snorkel filled the screen with a phone number at the bottom. "Anyone with information about the missing girl should call the Coast Guard."

"C'mon!" cried Brad to his brother, "Maybe we can find her and get a reward!" They jumped up from their breakfast and flew out the door.

~~~

The Coast Guard helicopter flew low over the Tolomato River, past the pier. It turned and flew over the inlet to the Atlantic Ocean and went North. "Nothing, Sir." The pilot radioed his commanding officer, who was waiting for news with Snorkel's dad and Uncle Rob. "We've been up and down the estuary and along the shoreline North and South. We haven't seen anything. She could be somewhere along the canals. We haven't given up. There's just so much coastline to cover."

~~~

Brad was the first to see it, lying upside down on the beach just past the pier. He waved to his brother, and they pulled in closer to the beach. Overturned on the beach was a blue kayak just like Snorkel's. "It's gotta be Fish Face's kayak," he said pulling out his cell phone and dialing 911. Then the boys beached their jet skis to wait. Brian walked up to the kayak. "Poor Fish Face," he said, and started to turn it over. "Don't touch it!" yelled Brad. "You'll get fingerprints on it. They might think we did it!" By the time Officer Martin and Sean ar-

rived, a group of people stood around the kayak.

"It's just like Snorkel's," said Brad to Officer Martin. "We didn't touch it in case it's evidence." Sean pushed through the crowd and turned the kayak over. There was no hand-painted "S" on the bow! "It isn't Snorkel's," he gasped with relief. Officer Martin spoke on his phone to a chopper pilot overhead. "It isn't the girl's kayak, Raymond. Continue to search along the coast." "Aye, aye, Sir," said the pilot. "Thanks, boys," said Sean to Brad and Brian Bucy. "Keep up the good work," said Officer Martin.

~~~

Two teenage boys in wet suits and carrying surf boards walked along the morning coastline. The waves were high after the storm— perfect for catching a good ride. Suddenly, one boy pointed up the shoreline. About a

hundred yards up the coast something had washed ashore and was
foundering in the waves. They
ran toward it. It was a rubber
raft. They caught it and dragged
it out of the breaking surf onto
the sand. When they looked inside, they found a black woman
with dreads, lying in the bottom,
unconscious. One of the boys
knelt to help her and felt her
pulse. She was breathing. She
was alive! They spoke quietly and
then the other boy ran up the
beach for help.

Chapter 16:
Figaro Ties a Perfect Bowline

Matilda's snout broke through the surface of the water. "Try this, Snorkel. It's my favorite," she said offering Snorkel a strand of seaweed with her prehensile lips.

"Thanks, Matilda. I've had seaweed before, like nori and wakame. What kind is this?" asked Snorkel.

"Turtle grass," replied Matilda. "It's delicious." Snorkel put the salty seagrass to her tongue to taste it.

"Snork, wait! I could get you some nice glass minnows or sardines or herring to go with it," cried Figaro.

"That would be great, Figaro. I could make sushi."

With that, Figaro dove into the great blue water and came up with a pouch full of tiny fish, which he deposited on the kayak. "Glass minnows," he said excitedly. "You put them on pizza," he added as an explanation.

"Anchovies! Right!" said Snorkel, grabbing some before they flopped off the kayak. She wrapped a tiny one in the turtle grass and popped it in her mouth.

"I personally love them on pizza," said Figaro. "But these are fresh."

"Not bad," said Snorkel. "It could use a little soy sauce. But it's not bad." She stopped and looked at her friends. "Thank you guys. I'd starve without you. You're the best friends ever!" She wrapped another anchovy in seagrass and popped it in her mouth.

The sun shone brightly on the ocean. Snorkel was still paddling, but she was slowing down. "I don't know how much longer I can keep going," she said. "I'm so tired."

"When I'm tired, I eat," said Matilda, offering Snorkel more seagrass. "It always revives me."

"Thanks," said Snorkel. "But I'm so sleepy, I can barely keep my head up."

Figaro dove under her chin to try to hold up her head. "You can't stop now. The current will pull you back out," he warned. "I'll just rest a minute," Snorkel said, putting her head down on the bow of the kayak. And she was out. No matter how Figaro flapped his wings, jumped up and down or called out, "Snorkel,

Snorkel. Look at me. There's no time to sleep." She slept. Even diving into the water to splash her didn't work. He landed in the water behind the kayak and tried to push it with his beak. "It's no good," he sighed.

"Wait," cried Matilda. "I have an idea!"

"Anything," said Figaro.

"Toss me the line on the bow of the kayak. There's a loop on the end of it. We can slip it over my bad flipper, and I can pull the kayak."

Figaro looked on the front of the kayak for the rope. He picked it up with his beak. "Is this it?" he asked. Matilda nodded. "There's no loop," he said.

"Well, we'll have to make one," said Matilda.

Figaro flapped his wings at her then lifted each foot. "No thumbs!" he shouted. "Not prehensile. You, dear, are the one with prehensile lips."

"Yes, but I can't tie a loop," she countered.

"Here, take this." Figaro gave Matilda the middle of the rope to hold in her mouth. "I live on a pier. I know how to make a bowline." Figaro grasped the end of the rope in his bill. "Wait. Does the rabbit go down the hole first or come out of the hole first?" He seemed puzzled.

"Whatever are you talking about?" questioned Matilda.

"The Nature Scouts. They come to the pier to learn sailing knots," he retorted. "Oh yes. I remember." He began to say and do the strangest things. "Here's the rabbit hole and here's the tree. Up through the rabbit hole, 'round the big tree; down through the rabbit hole and off goes he." As he recited the poem, Figaro made a rabbit hole with the rope by laying it in a loop on the water. In a flash, he dove under and came up through it sputtering, "up through the rabbit hole." Then he flew around Matilda and the bit she was holding, "round the big tree." He shot straight up into the air, and turned saying, "back through the rabbit hole, and off goes he!" Making a huge splash, he dove through the looped rope. When he surfaced, he pulled on the end of the rope. It was a perfect bowline.

"That was amazing!" exclaimed Matilda. She rolled over to lift her flipper stump. Figaro tossed the bowline loop right over it. "Great. Now I can pull her in." Matilda swam with her good flipper and tail and pulled the little kayak with Snorkel sleeping soundly in it. "How about a little travelin' music?" she requested.

"I'm bubblin' along," began Figaro. "From river to sea...and sea grass gives me sea gas, bwpp, bwpp, bwpp, bwpp." He made fart noises. "Hey, that would give you some propulsion." The little trio moved forward as the sun crested and Figaro sang, "Smelly, smelly fish heads are best. Jelly, jellyfish give me indigestion."

Chapter 17:
Meanwhile, Elsewhere

An ambulance reached the beach where the boy waited with the unconscious woman. The EMTs checked her pulse and administered oxygen. Then they lifted her onto a stretcher and carried her away, to the whine of a siren.

~~~

Grandpa cleared the plates from the table while Sean sat staring into the distance. "You know, you have to get some sleep, son," Grandpa said gently. "Everyone's doing their best. I believe they will find her."

"I don't know, Pop. I just can't lose Snorkel, too." He hurried out the door so his father-in-law wouldn't see him cry. The moon was full. "Maybe if Snorkel could see it," he thought, "she could find her way home."

~~~

The three friends moved slowly through a calm sea, under the high, bright moon. Snorkel still slept, Matilda pulled the kayak, and Figaro perched aft to balance the slight craft and to keep Snorkel from falling out. There was only the tiny trio, the full moon and a vast ocean.

Chapter 18: Encounter with Right Whales

Dawn rose over a glassy sea. Matilda still pulled the kayak with Snorkel and Figaro heaped together, snoring. Suddenly Matilda broke loudly into song. "I wanna rest my head on my underwater bed..." Figaro startled awake. "I'm a tired bovine in the water."

"Enough," coughed Figaro. "I can't stand that song anymore." He blew a few fart sounds. Matilda was starting to protest when the kayak was upset by a massive dark wave that tossed Snorkel into the water. Matilda was thrown too and got tangled in the line. Figaro, who was tossed high in the air, screamed. "Bird overboard! Girl overboard! Snorkel overboard."

Snorkel sputtered awake in the water. She had her life vest on, but the water churned violently. "Snorkel, are you okay?" Matilda called out.

"Yes. Just startled. What happened?" Snorkel asked. She grabbed onto the kayak as a huge gray wall rose out of the water just a few yards away.

"Hey! Cut that out!" yelled Figaro to someone or something no one could see. "Can't you see we've got a child here?" A small Right whale, about 30 feet long and weighing two tons, breached again and flopped over on its back. "Holy mackerel," called Figaro. "It's a Right whale!"

"Oh. It's only a little calf—just a baby," cooed Matilda. "It's hardly bigger than I am."

"If that's a baby, I hope Mama isn't with him!"

Snorkel was really awake now, clinging to the side of the kayak. "Wow!" she shouted. "This is the most incredible thing ever! You know Right whales are endangered?" Just then the mama whale rolled over and flapped her flipper several yards away. The water undulated. It looked like a blanket being shaken out.

"Not as endangered as we are right now," quavered Figaro.

"Hello! Hello! Ms. Right Whale, hello!" called Snorkel excitedly, pulling herself up onto the kayak to get a better look.

"Snorkel! Leave well enough alone," cautioned Figaro. "A wrong move and we're Ahab." Matilda flashed him an eye roll.

"What?" countered Figaro. "People tell stories while they whale watch from the pier. The things I've heard!"

"Right whales don't eat pelicans," responded Snorkel. "Or manatees or humans. They eat zooplankton. There are only 500 left on the planet," she went on. "Eighty-three percent of them have been injured by some sort of deep sea fishing gear." (9)

"Snorkel" urged Figaro. "This is not the time for an ecology lecture. That mama is 60 feet long if she's an inch, and on the back side of 80 tons. I don't think..."

Just then the baby whale breached again, and the mama whale surfaced. She shot up a huge, V-shaped spout of water that rained down on the trio. Figaro flew straight up into the air and out of sight. Water dripped off Snorkel's curls. The mama swam closer and rolled a single eye menacingly. Without opening her mouth, she spoke through her huge baleen teeth—otherwise she might have sucked them all in just from the motion.

"Didn't mean to scare you folks," she began. "Elrod was just curious about this strange mess floating out here. I didn't want him comin' over. Thought you might be draggin' lobster nets. But I couldn't stop him." Elrod surfaced, shot a smaller spout of water and noticed Snorkel clinging to the kayak.

"What are you?" he queried. "Are you some kind of mutant octopus?"

"She's more dangerous than that," answered his mama. "She's a human. They kill whales. They kill everything. I could tell you how thousands of our kind were slaughtered just to light some lamps. But it's too horrible." Elrod moved back toward his mother.

"I know about the whaling," offered Snorkel. "I'm so sorry. My kind can be thoughtless and very cruel.

Oh....I should have introduced myself. I'm Snorkel McCorkle, human. These are my friends Matilda and..." She looked around and saw Figaro high overhead. "And Figaro."

The mama Right whale turned her huge head and gave Snorkel the eye, again. Her eye was all anyone Snorkel's size could see up close. "You're odd for a human," said the whale. "Maybe one of these shiny things is a harpoon."

"No. No." retorted Matilda, moving protectively between the mama Right whale and Snorkel. "She's a human. I'll give you that, but not the dangerous kind. She's my best friend."

Mama whale gave Matilda the eye. "Is that so?" she challenged.

"Yes," countered Matilda, confidently. "You're pretty far away from home, human," asserted the ocean giant. "What are y'all doing this far away from shore in a little boat? They whaled in little boats like this."

"Oh no! Nothing like that. Snorkel, ah well, she was helping me find my missing flipper," Matilda rolled over to show her stump, "But a storm came up and dragged her kayak out past the pier and into open water."

Figaro floated back down to the bow of the kayak and puffed up protectively. "Right," he concurred. "Then this ridiculous mast Snorkel concocted came crashing down on her wee head and knocked her right out."

"And they've been helping me get back home," Snorkel chimed in.

Elrod came in for a closer look. "Mama, this Snorkel is the strangest creature I've ever seen. What's that growing on her head?" Of course her snorkel and mask were tangled in her hair.

"Never mind, Elrod. If these two fools are vouching for her, I guess this one is harmless." She turned and swam off a little distance, with Elrod following. Then they dove in unison, shaking the trio again when they lifted and flapped their huge tails.

"Of all the times not to have my camera out," lamented Snorkel. "I'll never be able to tell my Dad about this."

Chapter 19:
The Noise that Kills

Sean and Uncle Rob piloted the small outboard motor boat through the marsh canal looking for any signs of Snorkel. "This must be the one Snorkel video-taped," said Sean as they passed an ibis nest. "Why wasn't I paying attention? Why wasn't I home?"

"You can't blame yourself," his brother responded. "Snorkel's smart and she knows these canals and the rivers. If her kayak is damaged, she might be trying to repair it, heaven knows. She could be in someone's dumpster looking for duct tape. And the chopper pilots can't see her."

"I know she's smart and re-sourceful. But so was her mother...."

his voice cracked slightly. "What if she's hurt?"

"We'll find her," Uncle Rob in-sisted.

~~~

Snorkel wrapped a minnow in a big strip of sea grass and gob-bled it down while Figaro skimmed above the water catch-ing more anchovies. Matilda had been grazing underwater on sea grass when she bobbed to the surface crying, "Ouch! It's horri-ble!"

"What's horrible?" asked Snorkel.

"That noise," replied Matilda astonished. "Can't you hear it?"

Snorkel shook her head. "I can't hear anything."

"It keeps going off like every few seconds. SKREE-BOOM!" Matilda demonstrated. "One, two, three, four, five, six, seven, eight, nine, ten, SKREE-BOOM. It's ear splintering. And now they're coming."

"Who's coming?" asked Snorkel.

Matilda pointed towards a large pod of dolphins, who were leaping out of the water. They were swimming rapidly in their direction, as they headed out to sea. The dolphins surrounded the kayak in no time.

"What's happening?" cried Snorkel. "Where are you going?" It was Snorkel's friend Polly from the canal. She stopped.

"We're trying to get away from the noise," explained Polly.

"What noise? Matilda said there was a noise."

"It's seismic testing. Can't you hear it?" asked Polly.

Snorkel shook her head.

Just then Polly's friend Molly stopped. "You have to turn around," she said to Snorkel. "Some oil ship is shooting seismic beams testing for oil. Everyone who can is fleeing—whales, dolphins, even cod." (10)

"It's been going on for hours," added Polly. "We lost some of our pod when it started. We were too close to where it was."

"What happened to them?" asked Snorkel.

"Some of them lost their hearing. Some got lost and beached. Some just died from the sharpness of the noise," answered Molly.

"Yes. It's so intense it gives you a serious brain ache. Then you die, or you forget to breathe and die," said Polly.

93

"That's horrible!" said Snorkel. "What should we do?"

"You have to go toward the morning light," said Polly. "You have to swim away from the shore. Just follow us." And the dolphins leapt out of the water and swam away.

"We have to go back out to sea," exclaimed Snorkel.

"But we can't," objected Matilda. " We've worked so hard to get this far. We have to get you home."

"Not at the risk of losing you, Matilda," declared Snorkel. "You heard what Polly said."

"Yes, but..." said Matilda and Figaro in unison.

"But nothing. There is plenty to eat, and I am safe with you. Sadly, you are probably not safe with me. Besides, Matilda, you're the one who told me three steps forward, one step back." They couldn't really argue with that.

"One more thing we have to add to our list to fix when we get home," shrugged Snorkel.

"We're with you, Snorkel," Figaro added, as the little group turned to follow the dolphins back out to sea.

Chapter 20:
The Mystery Woman

A doctor and two nurses surrounded the rescued woman's bed. She was still unconscious. She was on oxygen, IVs ran to her arms, and she was hooked to a heart monitor.

"Solo necesitamos vigilar a ella hasta que ella llegue. Si ella hace. ¿Hemos notificado a su familia? ¿Sabemos quién es ella?" asked the Doctor. *[We'll just need to monitor her until she comes around. If she does. Have we notified her family? Do we know who she is?]*

"No hay papeles o identificación en ella o en la balsa," answered the nurse. "La policía registró la balsa. Nada." *[No papers or ID on her or the raft. The police searched the raft. Nothing.]*

"Solo tendremos que esperar y ver." he said, breathing a deep sigh. *[We'll just have to wait and see.]*

~~~

The moon was high and bright, again, as the trio moved out to sea. As Snorkel paddled, she sang a mournful song.

How Will I Know
Sung by
Katherine Archer

"Beneath the ocean lives a tiny grain of sand, Tumblin' and turnin' on its journey toward dry land, yet so determined.

How will I know?
How will I know?
I started out a million years before the sun
somewhere in silence.
I have a voice now and a soul
that's just begun
To find its place in time.

How will I know?
How will I know
when I've arrived?
when I've arrived?"
Beneath the ocean
lives a tiny grain of sand
struggling to surface.
Tumblin' and turnin'
on its journey towards dry land, yet so determined.

Snorkel laid her head down on the kayak and closed her eyes. She soon fell sound asleep. Figaro helped Matilda put the line over her flipper stump. The trio traveled on in the moonlight.

~~~

The same moon shone over the back yard at Snorkel's house. Her dad stood on the deck looking up at it. "I wonder if you can see this moon, my brave little Snorkel? If you can, I promise we will find you." Just then his cell phone rang. It was a strange number. He answered it. "This is Sean McCorkle," he said, expecting someone from the Coast Guard. "Oh my god! My god. Where are you? We thought you were dead."

~~~

Snorkel's mom was awake and sitting up in her hospital bed. "I know you must have," she replied. "I'm in the Canary Islands."

"The Canary Islands...how did you...?" stammered Sean.

"I had a life raft. I guess I followed the currents. It was the

96

first land I came to. I washed ashore. Some teenagers found me," she continued.

"Are you okay? It's been... it's been three months! We just thought..." his voice trailed off.

"I just kept thinking I have to get back. I have to get back to you and to Snorkel. I have to help Snorkel grow up, and you don't know how to do her hair. I have such a story to tell you!"

"Oh, Kelsey." Sean's voice dropped. "I don't know how to say this."

"Say what?" asked Kelsey. "What's wrong?"

"It's Snorkel. She's missing. She was out in her kayak when a storm hit. She's been missing for two days. The Coast Guard is looking for her. Rob and I have been out looking and the neighbors, too. We haven't given up. She's a bright little one—just like her mom."

Kelsey flung the covers from her bed. "I'll be home on the next flight. We'll find her. I love you," she said.

"I love you, too! Hurry home."

Uncle Rob and Grandpa were sitting at the kitchen table drinking coffee and looking at maps of the rivers and canals when Sean burst through the door shouting, "You won't believe this! It was Kelsey on the phone. I just spoke with Kelsey!"

"What? Where is she?" they both asked at once, in shock.

"She was caught in the currents. Just like Snorkel thought..."

"Incredible!" said Uncle Rob.

"It's a miracle!" cried Grandpa. "Where is she?"

Sean told them everything he knew. "We have to find Snorkel," Sean said. "We can't let Kelsey come home with no Snorkel to greet her."

"We'll find her," reassured Uncle Rob.

"She has to know her mom's alive!" said Grandpa.

97

Chapter 21:
A Dangerous Rescue

Uncle Rob's cell phone beeped, and he pulled it from his pocket.

"What is it?" asked Sean.

"It's nothing. Just a message I get when Snorkel's manatee is on the move." He put his phone down. "It's been going off a lot lately. I should turn it off, but I don't know how. Snorkel had to download it for me."

"Snorkel's manatee?" asked Grandpa.

Rob shook his head. "It's a long story," he said. "When we went to the Lily Pond Zoo, Snorkel wanted to see the manatee rescue center. It seems she saw this manatee in the canal with a track-ing device, so we downloaded the app to track it." He picked up his phone to show Grandpa and Sean.

"You know Snorkel. She's friends with all the animals. She named this manatee Matilda and follows it around." Rob pointed to his phone. "This is Matilda's dot. See, you can track where she is and where she's been." Grandpa and Sean looked at the phone. Uncle Rob looked at it again. "That's odd," he said. "The manatee is about four miles offshore and five miles north of the inlet. She's never gone that way before. Look at her trail. She usually stays in the rivers and canals." He studied Matilda's trail carefully. "And look at this! Two days ago she went out to sea."

"There was a huge storm," said Grandpa. "The manatee might have wanted safer water."

"Right," mumbled Rob, still looking at his phone. "This may be crazy, but what if they're together? Snorkel and the manatee."

"Stranger things have happened," said Grandpa. "Kelsey just rode the currents to the Canary Islands."

"Let's go!" cried Sean.

"I'll call Officer Martin on the way," said Uncle Rob. "They can get a chopper to the coordinates."

~~~

Snorkel was sleeping. Matilda was pulling the kayak with Figaro flying above when a huge wind came from nowhere. It disturbed Figaro in the air as well as churning the water and rocking the kayak. Snorkel woke up.

"Hey! Hey! Hey! Watch it! Whatcha doin' that for?" Figaro shouted at something overhead.

"Figaro, what's wrong? Where are we?" asked Snorkel.

"We were headed home, but that big whirlybird is causin' a scene."

Snorkel looked up. A helicopter was coming closer to the trio.

"It's the Coast Guard!" she cried. She waved at the helicopter. Then she looked around at Matilda who was still swimming with the rope around her stump.

"Matilda, what's that rope on your shoulder?" Snorkel asked.

"It's your tie up line. When I put it over my stump, I can pull you, so we don't just drift. We move kinda slow, but we moved all night," explained the manatee.

"Oh, Matilda, you are such a good friend. I will help you find your flipper. We will find it. I know we will," said Snorkel as she took the rope from Matilda's stump. "How did you get this loop on there?" Snorkel asked about the bowline.

"I helped," snapped Figaro, while demonstrating. "The rabbit comes up out of the hole, goes around the tree, then goes back down the rabbit hole." He splashed back into the water.

Snorkel just looked at him bewildered. "What?" he chided. "It's a perfect bowline."

Scouring the water for the little kayak, the co-pilot spotted it bobbing in the water. "Look!" he called into his headset mic. "There's the kayak, with the girl,

the manatee and a pelican! It looks like the manatee is pulling the kayak with a rope. Now what is that crazy bird doing?"

As they flew closer, the kayak rocked perilously in the choppy water. As the helicopter pulled up, the pilot called out over a speaker. "Snorkel...Snorkel...Can you hear me? If you can, wave your arm."

Snorkel waved.

"Good!" said the pilot. "It's too dangerous to drop a rescue person and sling to you. The chopper is disturbing the water too much. I'm gonna lift up to keep the wind and wake down. But there's a boat coming. If you need me to get you, wave both arms over your head. Okay? Wave one arm now if you understand."

Snorkel waved one arm in confirmation.

"Some rescuers!" snarled Figaro. "They'll probably drown us in the process." The threesome bobbed and bounced in the water as the helicopter lifted. Snorkel's hair blew around her face and Figaro's feathers were ruffled. They couldn't hear the engine of the Coast Guard boat as it came into view and pulled near the kayak.

Snorkel's dad called out to her. Snorkel shouted back and waved, but nobody could really hear anything. There was so much excitement. A diver in a wet suit climbed down a ladder into the water and helped Snorkel climb onto the ladder. Her dad and Uncle Rob reached over the side to help her into the boat.

When she was safely onboard, the paramedics wrapped her in a blanket and checked her vital signs. She was a little weak—as well as hungry, tired, and cold—but she was okay.

Her dad lifted her up and hugged her. Then Grandpa and Uncle Rob joined in a group hug. "Oh, Dad," she said, and being Snorkel she charged right into her saga. "We were in a sea of plastic and rescued a turtle, and dolphins were escaping seismic testing and a right whale, a baby Right whale! Jumped right out of the water in front of me and his mama was huge…"

"Whoa, whoa, slow down a bit," said her dad. "We'll have plenty of time to hear all about your adventure. Now I'm just glad you're safe."

Just then Figaro, who had been hovering overhead, landed solidly on the rail. "Squawk, squawk, squawk," heard the men.

"It's okay, Figaro. This is my dad, Uncle Rob, and Grandpa," Snorkel said. Then turning to the pelican, she continued the introduction. "This is Figaro."

"How d'ya do?" said Figaro bowing. "Squawk," heard the men.

"Figaro pulled me out of the water when the mast fell on my head and….Oh, I wasn't going to tell you that." Then Snorkel remembered Matilda, who was still swimming alongside the boat. "And this is Matilda." The manatee waved her good flipper. "They helped me the whole time, and they were bringing me home." Then she addressed the manatee directly, "Matilda, this is Uncle Rob. Remember, he took me to the Lily Pond." Matilda nodded and burbled something unintelligible to the grownups. "That's right," replied Snorkel. "That's where we downloaded the app that tracks your Lipzz." Uncle Rob nodded back.

"Actually, Snorkel," said Uncle Rob. "That's how we found you. Well, erm, we found Matilda. The app we downloaded at the Lily Pond beeped to show me where Matilda was, and on a whim I thought you might be together, and you were!"

The Coast Guard hauled up the kayak in a net, along with all of the junk velcroed and bungee corded to the side. It was a shambles. "How could a child survive in this ocean on that wreck?" sighed Grandpa.

"With the help of my friends, Grandpa," gushed Snorkel. "My very good friends."

Snorkel's dad broke in, "Uncle Rob was right about you and your friend." Figaro gave him the eye. "Friends," he corrected. "And you were right about something else." He paused for a moment then beamed, "Mom's been found. She's on her way home!" Snorkel's eyes lit up. "Mom's alive!" she gasped, then she folded herself into her dad's strong arms and cried.

The boat headed for shore with Figaro settling back down on the rail and Matilda swimming in its wake. They were not going to leave her now.

Chapter 22:
TV Heroines

The next few days were a blur of reunions and TV crews. News teams surrounded the McCorkle house. They hung out behind the bougainvilla and had boats in the canal.

They wanted stories of Snorkel, the 10-year-old girl who had survived a storm in a kayak and three nights at sea. They wanted interviews with Kelsey McCorkle, the woman who survived three months in a rubber raft and traveled across the Atlantic on the currents. They wanted stories of Matilda, the manatee with one flipper who had pulled the missing girl through the sea.

"We have a fascinating story tonight," boasted the reporter standing in front of the Coast Guard Station. "The girl who has been missing since Saturday's storm was located on her kayak in open sea north and east of St. Augustine. Rescuers said her kayak was being pulled toward St. Augustine by a manatee."

"It was the darndest thing I've ever seen," recounted the co-pilot of the rescue chopper to the reporter. The channel ran the B-roll of his video footage of Matilda, with the rope over her stump, pulling the kayak while Snorkel slept. A headline scrolled across the bottom of the screen, "Manatee Rescues 10-year-old Girl."

"The manatee had only one flipper," marveled the co-pilot.

"The girl was pulled from the water by Coast Guard rescuers," continued the reporter. "Apart from being hungry and tired, she seemed unharmed."

Perched on the dock, Figaro watched the news story through the window of the pizza shop. "Manatee Rescues Girl!" Figaro exploded. "No mention of the pelican! Harumph. Anyway, there I am. There I am!" He flapped his wings crazily toward the screen. "I'm flying guard overhead!" He flapped and squawked at everyone close by. "Hey, everyone, that's me! That's me!"

He called over the rail to Matilda. "We're on the news! The TV news! You're a hero! Big close up of you pulling Snorkel."

Matilda looked up at him from the water below. "What's a close up?" she asked. Figaro was stupefied. "What's a close up? Are you kidding me? A close up is something you could use for a big handout...a whole slice...maybe even a whole pizza with anchovies."

TV crews jockeyed for position at Gate 4B at the Orlando International Airport. A reporter spoke into the camera for Channel 6. "We are waiting for the arrival of Kelsey McCorkel, one member of the four-person water survey crew lost three months ago in a storm off the Florida Keys." When Kelsey appeared at the gate, Sean and Snorkel raced to greet her. They hugged and laughed and cried, completely unaware of all the news cameras.

The Channel 6 reporter pushed up to the family. "How does it feel to be home, Dr. McCorkle?" he asked, "when everyone here thought you were dead." Snorkel piped up, "I knew my Mom was alive, because she's just that smart." The reporter was so startled he forgot to follow up.

The TV played in the living-room at the McCorkle house. The whole family was there to greet Kelsey and Snorkel and watch the televised reunion. They applauded as the reporter said, "Greeting her are her husband Sean and her daughter, Mary Elizabeth. Known as 'Snorkel' to her friends, she is the girl who was rescued by a manatee. Dr. McCorkle survived in a life raft eating seaweed and raw fish and drinking rainwater she collected in plastic bags. She was carried on ocean currents to the Canary Islands, where she washed ashore and was found by teenage surfers."

When everyone had gone, Snorkel showed her mom and dad the map she had used to track her mom's progress. Snorkel's mom touched the map and moved her finger up and along the marks and dates her daughter had made. Her eyes filled with tears. "This is brilliant, Snorkel," she said, proudly.

Her finger stopped at the last mark Snorkel had made just north of the Canaries. "See this mark; it's very near the place I washed ashore on La Palma Island," Kelsey said. "This is the beach where the boys found me. I have so much to share with you, Snorkel my smart, courageous girl!" And they talked into the night about eating seaweed and catching fish and rainwater. And how both a girl and her mother survived being lost at sea.

That night both her parents tucked Snorkel in and kissed her good night. As her dad closed the door, he saw her mask and fins hanging over the bed post.

Chapter 23: The Lost Flipper

Figaro was right: Matilda was a huge hero. She could barely swim alone in the river or the canal for all the Matilda watchers wearing T-shirts reading "St. Augustine: home of Matilda the Manatee" and bearing a bad likeness of Snorkel's dear friend. Matilda was so much of a hero that a marine mammal vet from FSU and a vet from Maine—who had previously made prosthetic legs for horses, cats and dogs—teamed up to make her a new flipper! Of course it made the national news.

The TV reporter stood with the camera operator in front of the manatee recovery tank at the Lily Pond Zoo. "In more news related to 10-year-old Snorkel McCorkle, the girl rescued by the manatee with a missing flipper"—the camera panned to show Matilda in the tank with Snorkel hanging over the side and Dr. Gwen watching—" the research and veterinary team at the Lily Pond Zoo have fitted the manatee, named Matilda, with a prosthetic flipper." Matilda waved her new flipper at the camera. Then she and Snorkel did their new handshake—slap front, slap back, slap front, slap heart, and then the sign for "Happy." Matilda blubbered to her friend. "I knew you would help me find my flipper. You're my best friend forever."

Snorkel's classmates watched the news story showing Matilda and Snorkel at the Lily Pond Zoo. All of the kids cheered, even Brad.

Snorkel and Matilda were both happy about Matilda's new flipper, but they hadn't forgotten what they had seen in the ocean. They had work to do. Snorkel showed her video of the plastic quagmire to her classmates. "We have to change this!" she declared to her excited class. Ms. Murray wrote the students' suggestions on the board. "We can make sure we pick up our trash," offered a girl. "Oh! Oh!...We can stop using plastic bags," chimed in a boy from the back. "We can pick up trash at the beach" called out another classmate from the front. "We can tell our parents not to use plastic bags" shouted another. The class had many good ideas. In the end, they formulated a plan, and decided to ask their parents for help carrying it out.

On Saturday, Snorkel's class patrolled the beach. They also walked the river banks, the roadways, and the canals collecting bits and pieces of plastic trash. When they were fin-ished they had a pick-up truck heaped full of garbage bags. They were stuffed full of Styrofoam and plastic—cups, bottles, spoons, shopping bags, six-pack rings, straws, fishing line—all of which they had found in the environment.

On Monday night, the students and their parents attended the City Commission meeting. The kids marched into the meeting carrying their garbage bags of plastic trash, while their parents carried signs reading "No More Plastic," "No Plastic Straws," "End single use plastic!" There was a huge commotion in the hall as the students emptied the bags in a huge pile in front of the Commissioners. The Mayor banged the gavel. "Order! Order! Who's in charge of this?" he demanded. Snorkel raised her hand. "Please take the podium," he called. "It's Snorkel McCorkle," whispered someone. "Yes....It's the girl who was rescued by a manatee!" confirmed someone else. And the room erupted again.

"Order! Order!" barked the Mayor banging his gavel. "Now then, what is your name and why are you disrupting this Commission meeting?"

"My name is Snorkel, um... Mary Elizabeth McCorkle," answered Snorkel.

"Of course," conceded the Mayor. "We all know who you are, Snorkel. Why are you here?"

"When I was pulled out to sea in the storm, I ended up in a garbage patch of plastic as far as the eye could see." Ms. Murphy had patched Snorkel's video into the Commission's system. The images appeared on their screen. "It was devastating," Snorkel continued. "I saved a small turtle that was trapped in netting. The sea animals can't survive in this human garbage and neither can we. We need to stop using disposable plastic be-

cause it's destroying our planet and all the living beings on it." A cheer rang out from Snorkel's classmates.

"We, the members of Ms. Murphy's 4th grade class, want a future for us and the planet with all of its amazing creatures. If adults can't find the courage to stop using plastic," she continued, "every two weeks we will fill this room with plastic we find on the beach, in the river, along the roads, in the marshes—until you do."

Her classmates broke into more cheers and whistles. Their parents applauded and cheered. "No more plastic! No more plastic! No more plastic!" chanted the crowd.

"Order! Order please!" The Mayor banged his gavel. The room quieted some. "Snorkel, you and your friends have made a good case. Thank you for all of your efforts. The Commission will now vote on the ordinance before us— abolishing single-use plastic in the city limits. All in favor, please raise your hands."

The five members of the Commission looked at each other. A black woman, a white woman and a Latino man raised their hands immediately. They looked at the two white men remaining. One slowly raised his hand. The last member of the Commission surveyed the room. He looked at the students, their parents, his colleagues, and the plastic heaped in the center of the room. Slowly he raised his hand. The vote was unanimous! The room erupted with applause and shouts of glee. Snorkel and her friends high-fived each other. Parents rushed to their children to congratulate them. Both of Snorkel's parents hugged her tightly.

~~~

Snorkel's theme song played in her head as she raised the sail on her new kayak. "So grab your snorkel and grab your fins. Get ready for a wonderful day to begin." Matilda swam alongside as Snorkel sailed past the pier. Figaro saw them and flew out to meet them. Together the friends sailed and swam and flew into the magic of a brand new day.

Snorkel McCorkle Reprise
Katherine Archer

Made in the USA
Monee, IL
18 October 2021